THE SILVER CAN

THE SILVER CAN

JERRY SUTPHIN

Library of Congress Control Number:		2019902695
ISBN:	Hardcover	978-1-7960-1981-0
	Softcover	978-1-7960-1980-3
	eBook	978-1-7960-1979-7

Print information available on the last page.

Rev. date: 03/06/2019

To order additional copies of this book, contact:
Xlibris
1-888-795-4274
www.Xlibris.com
Orders@Xlibris.com
792976

CONTENTS

PART FOUR
LOU'S STORY

PART FIVE
EVERYONE WANTS THE SILVER CAN

PART ONE

HOW IT GOT HERE

CHAPTER 1-1

THE STRANGER

At the edge of the desert was an old trailer. Some would call it a mobile home. On one side, there was a driveway that led up to the main highway. On the other side of the trailer, there was a clothesline strung between two poles. A thin middle-aged woman was busy hanging up her washing.

There were no trees or green vegetation in sight. The woman, dressed in slacks and a red-and-white checkered blouse, noticed a figure approaching from the desert. She watched the figure for a few moments then went back to the trailer and reappeared with some binoculars.

"Oh my," she said as she dialed the binoculars into focus. She then went back into the trailer and called the sheriff's office. The call went through, and Sheriff Justin Smith got the message from the dispatcher. He was in the area, so he took the call.

The woman in the meantime had her shotgun and was watching the stranger from inside her trailer. As the stranger approached her clothesline, she noticed two things: it was a man, and he was naked. When he got as far as the clothesline, he took one towel down and put it around his waist, and he threw a second towel over his shoulders. Then he sat on the ground with his back against one of the clothesline poles.

The sheriff pulled into the driveway and dragged his fifty-two-year-old body out of his squad car. He had his police uniform on, khakis with all the sheriff emblems on it and a light-brown cowboy hat. The sheriff was a tall, burly man with brown eyes and graying hair. He approached the trailer and knocked on the front door.

He heard "Come in" and went inside the trailer.

"Hey, Jean."

"Hey, Sheriff."

Justin Smith was a longtime resident of Tate Country and knew almost everyone.

"Where is he?" Justin asked.

"Out at the clothesline," the woman said as she pointed out the back window.

They watched him for a few moments, and then Justin asked, "Did you see any weapons?"

"No, Jean replied.

"You sure?

"Damn sure, he was naked and had no place to conceal anything."

"Well, I guess I'll go talk to him." Justin cautiously went out back with Jean and her shotgun close behind. In a loud voice, the sheriff said, "Hello, I am Sheriff Justin Smith. What's going on here, mister?"

There was no answer.

"Are you all right?"

Still, there was no answer.

"You got a name?"

"Water . . . could I get a drink of water?" the stranger replied.

Jean heard the man and went to get some water. Justin looked him over. The stranger was a white male in his forties with dark hair.

"Well, what happened to you?" Justin asked. Again, there was no response from the stranger. "I want to help you, but you have to give me some answers."

"I can't remember. I woke up in the desert, and I can't remember anything, not even my name."

Jean came back with a bottle of water and gave it to the man. He drank half and poured the rest over his face.

"That's the truth, Sheriff," the stranger said. "I wish I knew more. It's been driving me crazy."

Justin turned to the woman. "Jean, do you have some clothes I can put on him to get him back to town?"

Without speaking, Jean ran back into the trailer and emerged with an old T-shirt and some blue sweatpants for the man. Justin watched the stranger put on the clothes and noticed the stranger was not as sunburned as someone who would have spent all day in the dessert. With the man dressed, Justin judged him to be about five foot ten, at 180 pounds.

With the clothes on, the stranger got in the back seat of the squad car. Justin said goodbye to Jean, and off they went toward town.

Justin and the stranger rode in silence, the stranger in the back uncuffed. Justin finally broke the silence.

"Did the sun burn you?"

"A little."

"If you need something for the burn, I'll get you something."

"I'll let you know, thanks."

"Remember anything yet? Does anything look familiar?"

"No," the stranger replied.

"I got to make a stop up here. Some kids were drag racing, and I got a hunch who it is," Justin said as he pulled into the driveway.

Justin got out and started walking toward this old run-down house. Before he got to the front steps, a young man in his twenties came out on the porch. They exchanged some words, and Justin came back to the car. He got in and took off his hat and ran his fingers through his thinning hair.

"He's lying," spoke the stranger.

Justin turned and looked at the stranger. "How do you know that? How could you even hear us? Did you, honestly, hear us?"

"Yes, I could hear you."

"You must have damn good ears."

The stranger paused then said, "I just know he's lying."

"Well, I think he is too. But I can't prove it. I was just going to warn him anyway, but I hate it when they lie to me."

Justin got the squad car back on the road and thought a moment and asked, "If you could hear our little talk, tell me what we said."

The stranger leaned forward and said, "You asked him if he had been on Stone Road lately, and he said no. That was his first lie. His second lie came when you asked him where he was last Friday night. He knows he was racing on Stone Road last Friday night."

"Well, did you get some kind of lie detector implanted in your brain while you were out there in the desert?" Justin asked.

"I don't know. I can't remember, but when that guy lied to you, it was plain as day to me that he lied."

Again, they rode in silence. Justin was thinking hard. *What if this guy can tell when someone is lying? I got to test him a little.*

"Hey, stranger, are you hungry? Want some more to drink?"

"Yes, but I'm not dressed for any restaurant."

"Well, that's okay. We got the AC in the car, and I'll get it to go. Burger and fries and a cold drink, the all-American meal."

Justin pulled into a diner. "Be right back." Then Justin disappeared into the restaurant.

Ten minutes later, Justin reappeared with a waitress, both carrying paper plates of food and drinks in paper cups.

"Hey, stranger. This is Wanda. She's got your lunch," Justin said, and then the waitress went back to the restaurant.

The stranger drank and ate a bite of food and finally said, "Her name is not Wanda. If you are trying to test me, you can do better than that."

Justin took a bite of the burger and chewed it down, then he took a sip of his drink.

"Yeah, well, I wanted to see if this talent of yours is the real thing."

The two men sat in the squad car and ate their food in between their conversation.

"I want to ask you a few—no, I want to . . . I have to deal with facts. If I make a statement, you can tell me if I'm lying. What do you think? Just between us."

"What's in it for me?" the stranger asked.

"Well, if you are a walking, talking lie detector, I can use you in a murder case. We have a man in custody for a murder he says he did not do. You help me, and I will do my best to help you find out who you are and whatever."

"You are going to trust me?" The stranger laughed.

"Yeah, well, maybe."

"Sheriff, you don't know me. I may be a criminal. I don't even know my name. You're nuts!"

"Well, maybe, but I'm a little desperate. And I would like to know if this guy is guilty. We don't get too many murder cases."

"If I do this, will you take me out to the desert where I woke up this morning?"

"I sure will try."

"Okay, tell me something and get this test over," said the stranger.

Justin thought a moment then said, "I've been sheriff for ten years."

"False."

"I've been married for twenty-seven years."

"True."

"I have never been to California."

"Yes, you have," the stranger responded.

"You are good."

"Can't you do better than this?"

The sheriff thought for a minute.

"Well, that is good enough for me."

"Come on, Sheriff. If you are going to put that much faith in me, you should ask me something that only you know. Of course, if it is a true-false question, I still have a fifty-fifty chance of getting it right."

"Well, no more questions. The station is right here."

CHAPTER 1-2

THINGS DON'T MATCH UP

Sheriff Justin Smith pulled his squad car into the Tate County Correctional Facility with the stranger that wandered in from the desert. Justin stopped the car and turned to the stranger and said, "Let's keep this little secret between us. Most people won't believe it anyway, and I'll never win another election in this town."

"Okay by me," said the stranger.

"I'll put you in a cell next to this guy. His name is Pete Roberts by the way. See if you can find out if he did it, and if not, find out if he knows anything. Okay?" Justin then looked at the stranger. The stranger nodded.

"First, we'll get your fingerprints and see if we can find out who you are. Roberts is the only person we have in custody, and it is a small jail."

Inside the jail, they took the stranger's fingerprints. Justin told Officer Jones to put him in the cell next to the accused murderer.

"What are we booking him for?" asked Officer Jones.

"We are just holding him until we can find out his identity."

"Yes, sir."

Justin sat in his office and pondered his next move. He thought about how he could use the stranger's "talent." *Maybe I could become a famous detective who solves crimes.* Then Justin thought, *What if it doesn't work or the stranger loses his ability to detect a lie?* The daydream came to a sudden halt. *What the hell am I thinking? Wake up, stupid.* What the stranger said was true. A true-or-false question has a fifty-fifty percentage.

Officer Jones knocked on the open door. "Sheriff, that guy you brought in wants to see you."

"Okay, bring him into my office."

"You want him cuffed?" the officer asked.

"No. Just bring him in. Oh, did you get any result from the fingerprints?"

"Not yet, Sheriff," the officer said.

"Okay, just bring him in. And as soon as you hear something on those fingerprints, let me know."

Officer Jones brought the stranger into the sheriff's office.

"That will be all. Close the door on your way out," Justin said to the attending officer.

"Sit down, stranger. Well, did you find out anything?" Justin asked as he leaned forward, anticipating the answer.

"He's guilty. He did it," replied the stranger. "The knife he used is buried in his backyard."

"It was that easy? He just said he did it?"

"You have to ask the right questions," replied the stranger.

There was a knock on the door. "Come in," Justin said.

"Just came in, Sheriff," the officer said as he handed Justin the papers.

"Officer Jones, take a man and a metal detector and search Pete Robert's backyard for a knife."

"Yes, sir, I'll get right on it."

"Thanks. That will be all, and shut the door," Justin said as he looked over the papers.

"Well, let's see what we have."

There was a long pause as Justin read the papers.

"We know who the fingerprints say you are. But things don't match up," Justin said. "Your fingerprints match a guy that disappeared from a St. Louis hospital twenty years ago." Justin breathed a heavy sigh. "I don't know what to do with you 'cause if this report is correct, you are 106 years old, and you don't look 106."

Justin looked at the paper and finally said, "Well, I'll read this to you, and you can stop me if it rings a bell or you have a question, okay?"

"Go ahead," replied the stranger.

Justin started to read aloud, "Dr. Thomas Dunn, eighty-six, reported missing from St. Joe's Hospital, St Louis, Missouri on June 9, 1997. Dr. Dunn had suffered a heart attack. A search of the hospital and grounds found no trace of Dr. Dunn. Officials believed that Dr. Dunn had some help leaving the hospital because of his condition. There has been no trace of Dr. Dunn since his disappearance. Dr. Dunn was reported missing by his family on June 14, 1997. The state closed the case in 2002 and assumed Dr. Thomas Dunn is deceased. There was no body recovered."

Justin looked up. "Anything coming back? What were you a doctor of?"

"I don't know," the stranger said. "Is that me?"

"Well, the fingerprints match. And there is a photo, but it is hard to tell. The man in the photo is much older than you look now," replied Justin. "I got an idea. May I call you Dr. Dunn?"

"Dr. Thomas Dunn, is that me?"

Justin took out his cell phone and looked through his contacts. When he found the number he was looking for, he dialed it. "Hey, Fruitcake. This is Justin." He paused. "Yeah, the sheriff. Are you home? Well, don't go anywhere. I'm coming over and bringing someone you'll enjoy meeting."

CHAPTER 1-3

FRUITCAKE

Justin and the stranger pulled into the driveway at a small run-down house, and there on the front steps stood Fruitcake. He was bald with glasses. He had on a pair of tan shorts and a tank top that revealed his somewhat flabby belly but muscular arms. He appeared to be about the sheriff's age. Justin and the stranger got out and approached the house.

"Hey, Fruit, this is Dr. Dunn. Dr. Dunn, Fruitcake. Real name is Rick, but we call him Fruitcake."

The two men shook hands and said hello. Then Justin spoke, "You know that shrink you saw that hypnotized you? I want you to call him. The doc here seems to have lost his memory."

Rick looked at the doc and said, "Man, don't you have any clothes better than that?"

Justin looked them both over and said, "You're about the same size. Give him something decent to wear. When we found him, he was naked."

Rick laughed. "Now we're talking. Come in, help yourself. The bedroom is in the back. Take what you need, Doc. I'll look up the shrink's number."

The stranger looked around the dark and shabby mess of a house. Dr. Dunn followed a path that led to the back bedroom, and Fruitcake made the call then hung up the phone. "He's gonna call me back. Want a beer?"

"No," Justin replied.

"I'll have one," the stranger yelled from the back. A few minutes later, the stranger appeared wearing tan shorts and a tank top.

The sheriff and Fruitcake looked at the stranger, and finally, Fruitcake laughed and said, "I like it. Beer's in the fridge. Help yourself. Hey, let's get a pizza. What do you say, Sheriff? You're buying, right? After all, this is official business."

The stranger looked at Justin and pointed to his clothes. "It's all he had."

Then the stranger pointed at his feet. "Flip-flops."

"Okay, Fruitcake, you call for the pizza, and I'm going out to the car and check in."

"What were you doing naked?" Rick asked the stranger.

"I don't know. I just woke up in the middle of the desert naked and started walking," the stranger replied.

"Aliens—they land all the time in the desert. I saw 'em."

"Is that why they call you Fruitcake?"

"That and a few other things. Justin and I went to school together back in the day. He's an okay guy."

The three men sat, eating pizza and drinking beer. "I better call my wife and tell her I won't be home for supper again," Justin said and headed toward Fruitcake's phone.

As he was talking on the phone, Rick said, "Hey, Doc, I got this pain in my back. As long as you're here, could you take a look at it?"

"I'm not that kind of a doctor," the stranger said. "I'm a doctor of . . . of—oh, I can't think."

Justin got off the phone. "You remember something, stranger?"

"Yes, but it is not much. I am not a medical doctor."

"Fruitcake, you got a computer?" the sheriff asked.

"Hell no," Rick replied.

The phone rang. Fruitcake picked it up. "Yeah," he said and paused. "Dr. Bell, wait. I'll put the sheriff on."

Fruitcake handed the phone to Justin and went back to eating his pizza.

"Good, ain't it?" Rick said to the stranger.

Justin hung up the phone and said, "We got an appointment for tomorrow at ten. So I have to figure out what to do with Dr. Dunn until then."

"He can stay with me," Fruitcake spoke up.

The stranger looked at Justin and shook his head no slowly. Rick, who had been looking at Justin, looked over to the stranger. The stranger stopped shaking his head and just smiled.

"No, I'll take him into town," Justin said.

"Okay, but he is welcome here," Fruitcake said. "Besides I want to know what's going on. Don't leave me out of this."

"Well, we'll see, Fruitcake. I have a computer at home. I want to check some things out. Maybe I won't involve the department on this. The hypnotizing idea is sure to raise a few heads. Dr. Dunn, are you ready?"

"Yes, what are you going to do with me?" the stranger asked.

"I don't know, but I want to find out what you are a doctor of, as a start. And I am wondering if you have some relatives still alive in St. Louis."

The two men said goodbye to Fruitcake and headed toward town.

"I have to tell you something, Sheriff," the stranger said. "Fruitcake told me he had seen aliens land in the desert."

Justin shook his head in a disappointed way.

"And?" Justin asked.

"And he was telling the truth," the stranger replied.

"Oh boy," Justin replied. "Well, this is getting too crazy for me. And if I say anything, I'll be called a fruitcake too. And I'll never run for office again. I am going to take you to my home. Is that all right with you?"

"I think so, Sheriff," the stranger replied.

"When we get there, wait in the car. Give me a few minutes with the wife before you come in. I'll think of something to tell her. She won't believe the truth."

It was dark when Justin pulled his car into his driveway, and the stranger sat in the car until he heard Justin call. "Dr. Dunn, you can come in now."

Dr. Dunn got out of the car and walked into Justin's home.

"Dr. Dunn, my wife, Shirley. Honey, this Dr. Dunn."

"Hello, Mrs. . . ."

"Oh, just call me Shirley. Glad to meet you. What the heck, you're dressed just like Fruitcake."

"Dr. Dunn had all his belongings stolen, and Fruitcake helped by lending him some clothes. I volunteered to put him up for the night."

"Okay, Dr. Dunn, I'll show you to the guest room. It's upstairs. Follow me," Shirley said and led Dr. Dunn through the house and up the stairs. Dr. Dunn noticed the pictures on the wall and how lovely the home was.

"Justin said you ate,"

"Yes, we did. Pizza with Mr. Fruitcake."

"Yummy, there are some towels and whatever in the bathroom. Make yourself comfortable. Holler if you need anything."

"Thank you, and good night, Shirley."

"Good night, Doc. Can I call you Doc?"

"Yes, you may."

Shirley turned to find the sheriff standing there.

"Oh, you coming to bed, Justin?"

"Be right there, honey," Justin said. "See you in the morning," he whispered to the stranger.

*   *   *

Dr. Dunn, the stranger from the desert, woke up in a warm bed and felt refreshed and clean from his shower the night before. He got out of bed and put on the only clothes he had, the ones he received from a man called Fruitcake. He opened the door and walked down the hall to the kitchen. The sheriff's home was clean and friendly.

"Good morning, Doc. How do want your eggs?" Shirley asked. "Justin is on the computer. How did you sleep?"

"Ahh." The stranger cleared his throat. "How do you like your eggs, Shirley?"

"I like my eggs scrambled."

"I will have my eggs the same, and I slept fine, thank you."

"I got toast in the toaster and coffee on the stove. Help yourself," Shirley replied.

Dr. Dunn filled a cup and sat down.

"This okay?"

"Yep, no assigned seats here," Shirley replied.

The stranger looked over at Shirley. Last night, it was dark, and he was tired. And he did not get a good look at her. He had not noticed the woman at the trailer or the waitress at the place they stopped by to get a burger and fries. But this morning, he got a good look at Shirley in her blue jeans and white flowery top. Shirley was a touch heavy but in the right places.

Justin walked in. "Morning, Doc."

"Good morning, Sheriff," replied the stranger. "You and Shirley have a nice home here."

"Thank you, Dr. Dunn."

"Do you know anything more?" He paused. "About my case?"

"Ahh . . . nothing solid," Justin replied.

"You want me to leave the room?" Shirley spoke up. "You two have a secret?"

"Police business, honey, nothing personal," replied the sheriff. "I already called the office, and I informed them I was taking Dr. Dunn somewhere to get him some help."

They heard a car pull into the driveway. Shirley looked out and said, "It's that Fruitcake with his matching clothes of the doc. I should take a picture of this."

Shirley let Fruitcake in, and they all said their good mornings.

"What do you need, Fruitcake?" Justin asked.

"I want to go with you when you take the doc over to see Dr. Bell."

Shirley jumped right in. "Dr. Bell, the hypnotist?"

There was a quiet moment, then Justin spoke, "Police business, honey."

"Dr. Bell is a wacko," Shirley said in disgust.

"No, he's an okay guy," Rick said, defending Dr. Bell.

"Shirley," the stranger spoke, "I can't remember my past, and I am sure your husband has good intentions of helping me."

"This is getting interesting," Shirley replied. "We got Fruitcake—a genuine nutcase—a man that can't remember his past, and my husband the sheriff all going to see another wacko, the hypnotist Dr. Bell. I'm going too."

"No, you are not," Justin said firmly.

CHAPTER 1-4

DR. BELL AND THE G-MEN

Justin drove down the highway, heading toward Dr. Bell's office, with Fruitcake and Dr. Dunn in the back. Shirley was riding shotgun. Justin thought, *This is a mistake. I should not be doing this. Someone is going to see the police car in front of Dr. Bell's office. Maybe I better park out back.*

Dr. Bell had an office in the renovated old school. Justin and Rick had gone there for their formal education. Now the building was an office building.

Justin pulled around back, and there he was—Dr. Larry Bell, a middle-aged man in a worn-out suit, smoking a joint. He quickly broke the joint and started waving his hands to get rid of the smoke. Dr. Bell was a thin middle-aged man with a thin mustache and slicked-back hair. He looked like he could be selling snake oil at a carnival.

"Good morning, ahh, Sheriff. A little early, but that's okay," Dr. Bell said, trying to look professional. "Come on in. Hey, Rick, everyone."

They followed Dr. Bell into his office. Justin looked the office over. He remembered the high ceiling. There was a carpet on the floor, a desk, a few chairs, a bookcase, and some documents hanging on the wall.

Justin started introducing everyone. "Dr. Bell, you know Rick, Shirley, my wife, and this is Dr. Dunn. Dr. Dunn seems to have lost his memory. Can you help?"

"Who's paying for this?" Dr. Bell asked.

"Why don't you considerate it a favor to the county, or I could run you in for possession of an illegal substance," Justin replied.

Dr. Bell paused and said, "Okay, this should not take long. Come here Mr. . . . er, Dr. . . . er, Dunn, is it? Please sit down. Listen to the sound of my voice. I'll slowly count from ten down to one. Relax, listen to the sound of my voice, ten . . . nine . . . eight . . . you are getting sleepy, seven . . . six . . . five . . . four, you'll be under . . . three . . . two . . . one."

"Sheriff, this man is a fake," the stranger said.

"Now we can try something else," Dr. Bell said quickly. He grabbed a light from his desk and shined it in the eyes of the stranger. "Look into the light."

The stranger looked into the light and then bolted up from the chair, tripped, and fell to the floor. Justin grabbed him. "He's passed out. I'm going to lay him flat on the floor."

"I'll get some water," Shirley said. "Dr. Bell, where can I get some water?"

"Down the hall on the right," Dr. Bell replied.

"I'll show you, Shirley," Rick said. The two went off down the hall.

"Well, you must have triggered something, Bell," Justin said.

Rick came rushing back and threw a pail of water on the stranger.

"Gee, Rick, you got my rug all wet," said a mad Dr. Bell.

Shirley came back with a glass of water.

"He's coming to," Justin said. "Shirley, let me have the water." Justin then gave a sip to the stranger then picked him up and put him back in the chair.

"I remember . . . the light on my face when they came and took me," the stranger said.

Everybody started talking at once. "Quiet, everybody, quiet," Justin said, raising his voice. "Just begin at the beginning and tell us what you remember."

"The light . . . they came in the night and took me. They flashed a light in my eyes, and I just floated out of my hospital bed. They took me outside and went like the speed of light up in the sky. I was in a room on what I assume was some spaceship."

The stranger paused then said, "I'm telling the truth as I remember. I . . . am a professor of ancient history and earned a doctorate in ancient history. I guess some people just started to call me Dr. Dunn. I am not a medical doctor by any means. Oh my . . . I just remembered I have a son and a daughter. They must be worried sick."

"Take your time," Justin said. "What happened on this spaceship?"

"My family . . . what am I gonna do about my family? They must think I am dead."

"Dr. Dunn, this is 2017. You have been missing for twenty years," Justin said.

"Oh, oh." There was a long pause. "Okay, they took me, from what I was told, because of my studies. They wanted to know everything I knew. At first, I would not cooperate, and they made promises to get me to talk. I would not believe them, so they gave me the ability to know when someone lies. Then they promised not to kill me and give me back my youth."

"You would think they could make you talk or read your mind or do some space magic to get what they want," Rick spoke up.

"Well, maybe. What did they want from you that was so important?" Justin asked.

"They have lost some of their kind and wanted to recover the bodies and take them back to their home planet where they can honor them, as it is their custom. They think I had some knowledge to help them. They fooled me. The aliens said they would not kill me, but the aliens never said they would let me go. I had been a prisoner for whatever long they had me."

"Twenty years, they had you," the sheriff said. "Why did you want to go back to the desert? You asked me to take you back there."

"I was not the only human they had on their ship. Others are being held," Dr. Dunn added. "I escaped . . . It might be too much for my family to see me like this. It's a shock for sure."

"How many others?" Justin asked.

"Two, an Englishman and a Russian. Both had been there longer than me," replied Dr. Dunn.

"Let's go get 'em, Sheriff!" yelled Rick.

"Shut up, Fruitcake. I have no idea what we are up against."

"We better get the government in on this," Shirley suggested.

"I agree," Dr. Bell said, putting in his two cents.

"Well, now let's think this over," Justin said. "Dr. Dunn, what can you tell us? What do you suggest?"

The phone rang. Dr. Bell picked it up. "It's for you, Sheriff."

Justin took the phone. "Hello." There was a long pause, then Justin said, "Okay." Then he hung up the phone. "Well, they are watching us."

"Who, the space people?" Rick asked.

"No, the US government," Justin said. "They are coming in, and they just wanted to tip us off so no one panics."

Two men came in dressed in suits. The older man of the two spoke, "I am Mr. One, and this is Mr. Two. We work with the federal government. We have had Sheriff Smith under surveillance ever since we received notification that someone inquired about Dr. Dunn. Dr. Dunn is an old but open case, and everything about it is classified."

"We bugged this room when we learned about this meeting," Mr. One continued. "We all know there is no such thing as spaceships and aliens." Mr. One looked at Dr. Dunn. "Yes, I know that's a lie, but that is the official statement. And Mr. One is not my real name, but we have to play the game."

"Mr. One, are we in danger?" asked Shirley.

"Wait a minute," jumped in Rick, "how do we know this is on the level?"

Then they all looked at Dr. Dunn. The stranger looked up and spoke, "He is telling the truth."

"Well, what now, Mr. One?" Justin asked.

Mr. One wiped his lips then stroked his chin. He was a man in his fifties who looked like he had seen it all. "We have to contain this incident. Which means all in this room must keep this to themselves."

"I won't say anything. You have my word," spoke Dr. Bell.

"Me neither," said Rick.

Shirley went over to her husband and put her arms around him. "What about Dr. Dunn and the two men on the spaceship?"

"Dr. Dunn is a victim here," Justin added.

"Two men on the spaceship? We did not know about the others on the spaceship. We need to debrief Dr. Dunn and learn all we can. We don't think they are a threat to the nation, but they have the power to hurt us humans."

"Can't we help my friends?" Dr. Dunn asked.

"Ahh," Mr. One stroked his chin and wiped his forehead. "This is complicated."

"Well . . . maybe we should . . ." Justin started to say.

"It's okay, Sheriff," replied the stranger. "He is telling the truth."

"Mr. Two, please take everyone outside while I speak with Dr. Dunn."

"Yes, sir. Okay, everyone outside," Mr. Two spoke for the first time. He looked twenty years younger than Mr. One. He was the muscle for sure. Mr. Two looked like a linebacker from Nebraska.

As they left the building, Justin also noticed a shiny black van parked at a distance.

"What d'ya think, Sheriff?" asked Rick.

"Yeah, honey, what's going on?" asked Shirley.

"Well, I think Mr. Three and Mr. Four are in that black van over there," Justin replied. "I think we are at the mercy of Mr. One."

"What are they going to do with us?" asked Shirley.

"Well, I don't know. Mr. One might just let us go. Dr. Dunn, on the other hand, might be in trouble beyond anything we can do."

"Shit, I kind of like the guy," said Rick. "Oh, here they come."

The two men came out of the building. Mr. One stopped to talk with Mr. Two, and Dr. Dunn came over to the group.

Dr. Bell, who had been silent, spoke up, "Look, I don't want no trouble. I don't want to go to jail. I want to go somewhere safe and have a smoke."

"Me too," said Rick.

"Yeah, and we know what you want to smoke," added Shirley.

"Well, Dr. Dunn, what is going to happen here?" Justin asked.

"I told him everything I know and—"

"Wait a minute," Shirley interrupted Dr. Dunn. "Justin, look at Dr. Dunn. He doesn't look right."

Justin, Fruitcake, and even Dr. Bell all went over and took a good look at Dr. Dunn.

"Shirley's right, Sheriff," Rick said. "He is looking older than he did this morning when I first saw him."

"I can't tell," replied Dr. Bell.

"Well, I think you are right, Fruitcake," said Justin. "How are you feeling, Doc? By the way, how did you escape?"

"Old trick. I bunched up the clothes I had on in my bed. I knew we were on land somewhere, so I sneaked around to the main door, turned off the alarm, opened the door, and went outside. I think the door closed automatically, and the fresh air and the sun just hit me. I just started walking, and my brain was on fire. Then I came to that place where you found me."

"That is why you were naked?" asked Rick.

"Yes, I guess so," answered the stranger.

"Hey, Doc, can you hear what they are saying? Use that talent of yours. See if you can—" Justin stopped talking because the stranger put his hand up in front of the sheriff's face.

The stranger had an intense look on his face. There was a long silence. "I can hear them . . . shhh."

The little group watched the two men with the fake names. Then Mr. Two walked to the van. Mr. One pulled a phone and made a call.

"What the—" Rick started to talk.

"Shhhh . . ." the stranger quickly hushed Rick. Then the stranger started to cry, "They knew, they knew, they knew all along!"

"What? They knew what?" all in the group were asking.

"Shhh, quiet," Shirley whispered. "Mr. One is coming."

The group quieted down. Mr. One approached the group.

"You knew. The government knew where I was the last twenty years. And they knew about the aliens and what they wanted," cried Dr. Dunn, confronting Mr. One.

Mr. One rubbed his hands then his chin. He then gestured with his hand. "It's complicated." Mr. One continued, "I don't make the decisions. I follow orders. I have priorities that I must follow, and sometimes people are collateral damage. Sheriff, I have to ask you for your weapon."

"Don't do it!" yelled Rick. "Run for it. In the car."

Rick, Shirley, and Dr. Bell all ran and jumped in the squad car. Justin and Dr. Dunn held their ground. Mr. Two came running. Mr. One held up his hand to stop Mr. Two.

"This is not necessary, Mr. One," said Justin. "There will be no gunplay or need for violence of any kind. We all want a peaceful solution."

Shirley got out of the car and stood by her husband's side. Rick and Dr. Bell lit up a joint in the back seat of the squad car.

"Okay, I am listening," Mr. One said as his hands rubbed his side and then his pants.

"Well, I think we should hear what Dr. Dunn has to say," Justin said.

All eyes turned to the stranger that walked in from the desert.

"I heard you, Mr. One, talking on the telephone. The incident in Roswell in 1947 when the alien spaceship crashed set off this search that these aliens have been on for seventy years, trying to recover the bodies of their lost kin. You know they thought that one of the two men they had kidnapped or I could help them."

Dr. Dunn paused then continued, "It is true I have been in the pyramids in Egypt, to the jungles of South America, and other places of so-called UFO activity. But I did not know where these bodies were, but you did, the US government did."

"Let me make a phone call," Mr. One said. "You are not going anywhere, are you?"

"No, sir," they all agreed.

"You, Dr. Dunn, turn around and plug your ears," Mr. One gestured with his hand. He then walked away and pulled out his phone. Fruitcake and Dr. Bell got out of the car and joined the others.

"What's going on, Sheriff?" asked Rick.

"Well, this is so stupid. Why are they trying so hard to keep this a secret?" Justin answered. "The bodies the aliens are looking for are being held by the US government."

"Seventy years," Shirley said. "They have held those bodies this long. There can't be much left of them."

"Man, is that what they want? Give them the bodies. Trade them for the two on the spaceship and be done with it," added Rick.

"Hey, everybody. Look at Dr. Dunn," Dr. Bell spoke up. "The doctor doesn't look so good."

They all went over to Dr. Dunn. He was aging before their eyes.

"We have to do something," Shirley exclaimed.

"Maybe he will stop aging if you get to get him back on the spaceship," Dr. Bell suggested.

"Well, you might have something, Bell," said Justin.

Mr. One put his phone away and walked over to the group.

"Hey, Mr. One. Dr. Dunn is dying!" Shirley exclaimed.

He wiped his lips, then Mr. One spoke, "I was afraid this would happen. The longer he is out of the ship, the faster Dr. Dunn will age."

Dr. Dunn came over to Mr. One. "I don't want to go back on the ship. What little time I have I want to use to see my children in St. Louis."

Mr. One put his hand over his eyes and said, "Okay, I'll make another phone call."

"Well, now wait a minute. Is there a reason why you or the government can't give the bodies back to the aliens? Would that not clear a lot of things up?" Justin said. "The government has had them for seventy years."

Mr. One rubbed both his hands over his hair. He thought for a minute. "Mr. Two!" he yelled and motioned for him to come over. After a brief private conversation with Mr. Two, he then turned to the group. "The remains have deteriorated, and they are no good to anyone anymore. No one has asked about them in years." Mr. One then put both hands on the top of his head. "Things do come up missing. What do you think, Mr. Two?"

"Whatever you say, Bob, I mean, Mr. One. I personally hate this assignment."

"Okay, Sheriff, I have a plan, and you can call me Bob."

CHAPTER 1-5

THE HOME BUTTON

Sheriff Justin Smith took a hard look at this man who just said to call him Bob and said, "Why are you doing this, Bob?"

Bob put his hand up toward his chin and gave it a rub and said, "I don't know why we are working on a twenty-year-old kidnapping case when we have known where he was for years. We have three intelligent young men, who are highly trained and highly skilled, wasting all their talent on this stupid case. It is time to close it and reassign these guys to something where they can use their skills."

"Well, what about you, Bob?" asked Justin.

"I can retire, if they don't nail my ass to the wall," Bob replied. "Okay, now, this is what we do." Bob reached into his pocket and started to write on a small card. "Sheriff, you go to this location. I'm sure you know where it is. I will call ahead and have someone waiting for you with a vehicle more suitable for the desert. I'll have them set a GPS that will take you to the spaceship. Yeah, we know where it is. Take Dr. Dunn with you. He may be the key to getting the aliens to cooperate with the exchange if the other two want to get off the ship. They may not want to once they know that they will age fast and die."

"Ok, I got it," replied Justin.

"I'll put these young men to work by getting the remains of the bodies and meeting you at the ship." Bob started to walk away, then he turned and said, "We'll be coming in on a chopper." Bob looked over at the group. "How is Dr. Dunn doing?"

"He looked forty this morning. Now he looks seventy," Shirley said.

"Yeah, he is fading fast," Rick added.

"You better hurry," Bob said to Justin.

"Well, let's go," Justin said. Everyone jumped in the car except Dr. Bell.

"Ain't you going, Bell?" asked Rick.

"No, I have had enough excitement. Good luck," Dr. Bell said. "And nothing personal, but I want no part of this."

Justin had the squad car on the road, speeding to its destination.

"What do you think Bell meant by that?" Rick asked.

"Don't know, and I don't care," Justin replied. "Doc, how are you feeling?"

"A lot weaker than I thought I would. My head is on fire again."

"Feel his head, Fruitcake."

"Yeah, it's hot," replied Rick.

"What do you think, Shirley?" Justin asked.

"We could try some ice," Shirley said.

"Right up here, you can get a bag of ice for a dollar," Rick said.

Justin slowed down and pulled in and stopped the car.

"Go in and get a bag, Fruitcake, hurry."

"You got a dollar?" Rick asked.

Justin put the car in park, jammed his hand into his pocket, and pulled out some bills while yelling, "Fruitcake, one of these days I'm gonna kick your—"

Fruitcake grabbed the money and flew out of the car and into the store.

"Calm down, dear," Shirley said. "You know how he is." She then turned her attention to Dr. Dunn. "I'm getting in back with Doc. I can be more useful there."

Fruitcake came back with the ice, and the group went off again. Rick is now riding shotgun. Shirley, now in the back, used the ice to help cool the stranger down.

"What ya got in the bag?" Justin asked. "And where is my change? That one bill I threw at you was a ten."

"There were some cookies and candy bars by the cash register, so I grabbed some. I am hungry," Rick said.

"I am too," Dr. Dunn said from the back.

"Well, okay, open it up and pass it around. I guess we are all a little hungry."

"It has been a while since we ate this morning, dear," reminded Shirley.

There was silence for a few minutes as everyone gobbled down candy and cookies.

"Now I'm thirsty."

"Well, suck on some ice, Fruitcake," Justin replied.

"Hey, Sheriff, when we get where we're going, I got to go," Rick said. "You know, pee."

"Well, you are in luck because we are almost there," said Justin as he pulled in and stopped the car. Everyone got out. Fruitcake ran around the corner of the building. A tall man in slick Western clothes came over.

"Sheriff Smith?" he asked.

"Yes."

"Bob called. I have your vehicle gassed and ready to go. I set the GPS, and when you want to come back, push 'home' on it."

"Well, okay, sounds good."

"There is a phone in the vehicle, and here is a card with my number and Bob's number. Good luck."

"We'll be all right. What the hell am I thinking?" Justin said, as they headed out into the desert. Shirley was back to riding shotgun. Fruitcake had to help Dr. Dunn from the squad car to the Range Rover they were given to drive.

"We will be all right, dear. I have faith in you," Shirley said.

"You're a good woman, Shirley," said the stranger in the back seat. "You're a lucky man, Sheriff."

The group traveled on, then Justin stopped the vehicle.

"What's the matter, honey?" asked Shirley.

"Well, I was thinking. How did Bob know how to have that man back there set the GPS? What if the aliens let Dr. Dunn escape on purpose and we are doing just what they want us to do?" Justin replied.

"You think it's a trap?" asked Rick.

"Well, I am not sure. I'm not sure Dr. Dunn is Dr. Dunn. We have no idea how much power these aliens have. They could have somehow made his fingerprints look like the real doc's prints. This stranger could be faking whatever he is doing."

The three of them looked at the stranger in the back seat.

"He doesn't look like he is faking," said Rick. "He's been eating human food."

"Maybe he likes earth food," Justin said.

"I was sure he was checking out my butt this morning at breakfast," Shirley added.

"Well, you can't blame him for that, honey."

"I don't blame you for being suspicious," the stranger said. "Are you sure Bob and his people are who they say they are?"

The three looked at one another. "No," the three all said.

"We took your word for it," Shirley said.

"What do you think, Sheriff?" asked Rick.

"Well, Fruitcake, you said yourself you saw spaceships land in the desert," Justin said. "Were you telling the truth?"

Rick closed his eyes. "I may have been under the influence of a certain weed at the time."

Attention went back to the stranger. "You said Fruitcake was telling the truth about that, didn't you, Doc?" Justin asked.

"He was. He just doesn't remember," the stranger replied. The stranger then sat up and grew a little younger and stronger in front of their eyes.

Rick and Shirley both gasped. Justin lowered his head and said, "I thought the escape story was too easy."

"I do not want to frighten you," the stranger said. "Dr. Dunn died twenty years ago, before we could get any information from him. All we want is to recover our loved ones. One of those bodies was what you would call my grandfather."

There was a long silence. "Relax, I just want to show you what twenty years of our technology and research have produced." Then the stranger turned himself into a woman. Then a dog, and then back into Dr. Dunn. "Want to see what I really look like?"

"No," all three said together.

"You sure had me fooled," Rick added.

"Pretty good act. I was completely taken in," Shirley said.

Justin sat in silence.

"Fruitcake had a good word for it back in Dr. Bell's office—space magic. I did wonder why the aliens could not figure out where the bodies were. What about the Englishman and the Russian?" Justin asked.

"I made them up, hoping to use that story to get back to the ship. We have known for some years where the bodies are. They guard the place very well. So we came up with this plan."

"Don't you have the firepower just to go and get them?" Rick asked.

"That would be messy and draw a lot of attention that we don't want. We come here and visit, but we do not want to interfere with your way of life."

"What do you want us to do?" asked Justin.

"Play it out, and everything will be okay. We do not want to harm anyone. I am choosing to trust you three. I think you are good people. You have more to fear from Bob and his group than you do from me."

"Well, what do you two think?" Justin asked Fruitcake and Shirley.

"I think we should help the stranger," Shirley said. "I would want my loved ones buried proper."

"Me too," Rick said. "Then I really did see those spaceships land?"

"Yes, you did, Rick."

"I thought I was dreaming."

Justin started the Rover back up and headed toward the ship. They were only ten minutes away when they heard a chopper.

"How did you come up with this plan? You seem to be getting what you want," said Justin.

"I have been playing by chance. The fingerprints were in the plan because we thought that would get someone's attention, which it did, and the response was better that I expected."

"How do you want to play this, stranger?" Justin asked.

"Sheriff, you have to tell Bob I changed my mind and am staying with the ship. Rick, you will have to pretend to help me over to the ship. When the bodies are on board, we will close the doors and prepare for takeoff. As long as Bob and his team don't do anything funny, this will be over, and you can go back to your lives. Just in case I don't see you again, I want to thank you."

"Stranger, remember that guy I asked you about in the murder case?"

"The man in the cell. Yes, I do."

"Well, in all the excitement, I forgot to tell you. My officers found the knife in his backyard. It is believed to be the murder weapon."

"I do have perfect ears so that I can hear far away, and I do have some sensitivity that humans don't have. That is why I felt I could trust you with the truth."

The chopper landed, and Bob got out and started walking toward the Rover as it was pulling up.

"Rick, quickly, get me to the ship." As the stranger spoke those words, the ship became visible. It was a large silver sphere. "Hurry, I don't want to speak with Bob."

Rick and the stranger left in a rush and stood by the opening of the ship. Bob went to the Rover and spoke with Justin. "You have any trouble? How is Dr. Dunn doing?"

"Well, the doc is having problems and has decided to go back on the ship," Justin replied.

Bob rubbed the side of his head and said, "Just as well. He may not have made it back to St. Louis. My men are loading the bodies now."

They loaded the bodies, and Rick came back to the Rover. The ship went straight up and silently disappeared.

Bob rubbed his chin and said, "I should not tell you this, but we have waited years to get tracers on one of their ships. We can track those coffins almost anywhere in the universe."

"Did you know about Dr. Dunn?" Justin asked.

Bob put his hands on his hips then folded them across his chest. "That he died twenty years ago and that this alien was imitating him?"

"Yeah." Justin laughed.

"When I get out of here, just push 'home' on your GPS."

"Well, Bob, I think we will be all right. How do you want me to file this report?"

Bob looked at the ground and scratched his head. "That's your problem. I got my own paperwork to file." Bob reached out his hand. "Good luck, Sheriff. Push 'home,' and it will take you home. Wait till I get out of here first." Bob then waved to Shirley and Fruitcake before he turned and headed to the chopper.

Fruitcake stood there a minute then ran after Bob. "Wait. I got a question for you."

Justin and Shirley could not hear what Rick was asking Bob. They saw Bob wave both his hands at Rick as if to say "Get out of here." Bob then got on the chopper and was gone.

Fruitcake came back to the Rover and got in the back. Shirley and Justin climbed in front.

"Well, what was that about?"

"I just wondered if he knew who shot Kennedy," Rick said. "Seems like a reasonable question. Hell, I thought he might know."

Justin reached to push the home button but then stopped.

After a short pause, Rick asked, "What's the problem?"

"What is wrong, Honey?" Shirley asked.

"Bob said, 'When I get out of here push the home button.' He said it twice. He also said, 'Sometimes people are collateral damage.' Dr. Bell said, 'I want no part of this.' I wonder what he meant. If I touch this button and we blow up, that would get rid of a lot of loose ends for Bob and his boys."

A groan came from Fruitcake and Shirley.

"You think they would do that?" Shirley asked.

"Fruit, how well do you know Dr. Bell?"

*   *   *

At the edge of the desert was an old trailer. Some would call it a mobile home. On one side, there was a driveway that led up to the main highway. On the other side of the trailer, there was a clothesline strung between two poles, where a thin middle-aged woman was hanging up her washing.

There were no trees or green vegetation in sight. The woman noticed three figures from a long distance off, approaching from the desert.

PART TWO

THE DISCOVERY OF
THE SILVER CAN

CHAPTER 2-1

DEATH IN THE DESERT

Three months later, two young men were riding their motorcycles in the desert. They spotted a deserted Range Rover and stopped to investigate. The younger of the two saw a shiny object off in the distance.

"Hey, Dwayne, see that thing shining over there?" asked Eddie, the younger of the two brothers.

Dwayne looked up and saw the glimmer of something small off in the desert. He shrugged and said, "Probably a beer can."

"I'm going to ride over and take a look."

"Go ahead and waste your time. I wish I knew how to hot-wire this Range Rover. It has been sitting awhile, but it might start or turn over."

Eddie hopped on his motorcycle and rode over to the small shiny object. He got off his bike and picked up the object. It was the size of a beer can, but there was no opening. There were no markings, but there was some weight to it. It felt warm and good in Eddie's hands. He smiled and tucked his shirt in his pants and placed the silver can between his belly and his shirt and rode back to his brother.

"What did you find, Eddie?"

"Here, take a look," Eddie said as he tossed the can to his brother.

Dwayne looked the can over. He felt the weight and did not want to give the can back to his brother. Dwayne felt a feeling come over him. Dwayne started laughing.

"It looks like a piece of junk," said Dwayne.

"You are jealous because I found it."

Eddie started dancing around and laughing.

Dwayne was trying to hide his feelings. He wanted the can for himself.

"You are jealous, aren't you, Dwayne?" Eddie remarked and laughed while still dancing around.

"Come on, let's go. I'll race you back to the truck," Dwayne said as he got on his motorcycle.

Eddie took the can and tucked it back in his shirt, and the two brothers rode back to where their truck was parked. Eddie and Dwayne rode their bikes onto the truck, and Eddie put the can into his backpack in the truck.

Eddie looked at Dwayne and laughed.

"Eddie, let me see the can."

"No."

Eddie ran off into the desert. Then he came back and ran around the truck.

"What is the matter with you? Let me see the can."

Eddie ran around the truck and stripped off his cloths. Dwayne watched his brother and started laughing. Eddie finally stopped and fell over. Dwayne walked out to where Eddie lay.

"Eddie, are you all right?"

"I have an awful headache. Help me. I feel so weird. I feel so happy, but this headache is killing me. Dwayne, help me."

"Okay, Eddie. Let's put your pants on. I don't like picking you up when you're naked. It's embarrassing."

Dwayne helped Eddie back to the truck and then went out to pick up the rest of Eddie's clothes. When he returned, Eddie was lying still on the sand. Dwayne turned on the truck radio and cranked it up as loud is it could play. Dwayne started dancing around while looking for the can.

"What are you looking for, Dwayne?" asked Eddie, standing there with his hands behind his back.

"What do you have behind your back, Eddie?"

Eddie had a tire wrench and swung it and knocked Dwayne down.

"I can't stop this pain in my head. I can't stop this pain in my head," Eddie yelled while striking Dwayne over and over.

*   *   *

Sheriff Justin Smith was sitting at his desk when Officer Jones entered the sheriff's office.

"Sheriff, we have two missing young men. They were staying at the Green's Motel, and no one has seen them in three days. Their parents are in Austin, Texas, and have called us to investigate."

"Let me see the paperwork you have," said the sheriff. "Dwayne Passmore, age twenty-one, white male, six feet tall, one hundred and eighty pounds. He has blue eyes and blond hair. Edward Passmore, seventeen years old. I assume they are brothers."

"Yes, Sheriff, they are brothers."

"Edward Passmore, five feet, nine inches tall, weight one hundred seventy pounds. Same eyes and hair color as his brother. Missing three days you say, Jonesy?"

"That's right, Sheriff. The clerk at the motel says they went out into the desert to ride their dirt bikes and did not return."

"Did the two boys leave belongings in their rooms? And did the management at the motel believe they were returning?"

"They were expected back, Sheriff, but no one said anything. Being young, they could have been exploring or something."

"Well, I guess I better go over to the motel. Are these rich kids?"

"I don't know, Sheriff."

"Jonesy, see what you can find out about the family for me. Call me if it is something I should know."

"Okay, Sheriff."

Sheriff Smith pulled into Green's Motel and went to the front office. Juan Garcia, the owner, was at the front desk.

"I'm glad to see you, Sheriff," Juan said in a worried voice.

"Well, good to see you too, Juan. Fill me in."

"The two young men were staying here and should have returned. Their father has called me about ten times. He is upset, and I think he is flying out here."

"Yeah, we have had some calls at the office too."

The sound of motorcycles halted their conversation. The sheriff looked; it was Johnny Ramirez. Johnny and his fellow riders could be trouble. Justin never had anything he could pin on Johnny, but Justin knew Johnny was running drugs or something.

"Hey, Sheriff, can I see you a minute?" asked Johnny.

Justin walked out to where Johnny was by his motorcycle.

"Hello, Johnny." Justin did not feel comfortable around Johnny. Johnny was a big man in his forties, over six foot and stocky. He had scars on his face and arms from fights he had been in. Johnny also had six riders with him that could destroy this small town if they wanted to. "What can I do for you?"

"Me and my friends here, we don't want no trouble."

"Well, good. I don't either."

"One of my friends found a dead body out in the desert. I know we will be the first suspects. We did not do it. See, we are being good citizens and reporting it."

"Was it a young white man with blond hair? Maybe with a truck and some motorcycles?"

Johnny turned and looked at one of the riders. The man nodded, and Johnny looked back at Justin.

"Yes."

"We have two young men missing. They are brothers. They have been missing for three days."

Johnny turned and looked at one of his men. The man held up one finger. Johnny looked at Justin. "Only one dead body, Sheriff."

"You probably don't want to stop at my office and file a report, do you?"

Johnny looked back at his friend, who looked down.

"No."

"How about a location? Could you give me directions?" the sheriff asked.

Johnny again looked at his man. This time, Johnny got up and walked back to talk with him. After a short talk, Johnny came up to the sheriff.

"Can you keep us out of this? We don't want to be involved. But I will help you locate the truck and one of the bodies. You should hurry because that body has been cooking for a few days already."

"If you and your friends had nothing to do with what happened out there, you have nothing to fear. I'll try my best to keep you out of this."

Johnny laughed. "Damn, Sheriff, all right. You go to Kaminsky's garage and head north into the desert. Go ten to twelve miles, and you will find what you are looking for right about there. There is an abandoned Range Rover if you travel another three or four miles north."

Then Johnny and his biker buddies road off. Before Justin could call his office, Officer Jones pulled into Green's Motel. Justin walked over and talked with Jonesy as Jonesy sat in the squad car.

"I think we have a location, Jonesy," said the sheriff.

"That's good, Sheriff. The state boys are taking over the investigation. Captain Manuel Mendez is going to be in charge."

"That is for the best because we don't have the men or resources to deal with this. I know Manny. I'll give him a call."

CHAPTER 2-2

THE STATE TAKES OVER

Sheriff Smith waited at the Kaminsky's garage. The state police helicopter came into view and landed long enough for the sheriff to climb aboard. They spotted the truck with the motorcycles in the back and landed at the site.

"Thanks for letting me come along, Manny," said Justin.

"Thanks to you, Justin, we did not have to search the desert looking for the Passmore boys."

The two men walked to the truck. The stench of the dead body was overwhelming. Manny looked at the plate number on the truck. It was the Passmores' truck. Manny walked over to the passenger's side and found the body. With a handkerchief over his mouth, he fished out the wallet. He then walked back toward the chopper.

Justin looked at the truck. It had dents here and there. Someone had used something to pound on the truck. It was something that left long dent marks.

Justin walked back to Manny. Manny showed Justin the name on the driver's license. They had found Dwayne Passmore.

"Justin, I'm calling this in. We need more men and forensic people out here."

"Well, I'm going to wander out this way, Manny. Maybe I can find something."

"Okay, Justin, I'm going back to the chopper and wait for the crew to get here."

Justin walked over the sand dunes. He wondered how far it was to the Range Rover that Fruitcake, Shirley, and he had left in the desert. *How long ago was that?* he asked himself. Justin wondered if there were explosives in the Range Rover. He now realized it was not responsible to just leave it there. Someone could have come along, like those two young men, and set it off. Justin had to make it right before someone did get hurt. He turned to walk back to the chopper when he saw the other body. Justin walked in that direction and the smell became putrid. He saw the body was naked.

Justin saw something else in the sand. It was a bloody tire wrench. The blood was baked on the wrench. Justin saw Manny walking his way and motioned for him to come over where Justin was standing.

"What did you find, Justin?"

"Another body and what could be the murder weapon."

Manny looked the wrench over, careful not to disturb it.

"Yes, it could be. The boy at the truck was beaten with something. I would put my money on this tire wrench. We have some help flying here. Let's get back to the chopper. This smell is gonna make me puke."

Justin turned when he heard another chopper. Manny and Justin walked back to the crime scene. State police officers had landed and secured the scene. They were all busy doing their jobs. Justin knew it hurt a little when he had to turn over the case to Manny, but Justin also knew that his little office could not handle this crime scene.

Manny yelled over all the noise, "The other body is about five hundred yards to the north!"

One of the officers nodded.

"Thanks, Justin, you have been a big help," Manny said.

"Well, I did not do much."

"You saved us a lot of time. That was a good tip you had. Want a ride back to town?"

"Manny, there is a Range Rover abandoned about half an hour north of here. There is a rumor that there are explosives in it. Could you check it out or blow it up? I don't want someone to get hurt."

"What was that about?"

"Manny, you would not believe me. I was out there with someone I did not trust, and they left me and the Range Rover. They told me several times to push the button for the GPS and it would take me home. I was not sure which home they meant. So after they left, I walked out of the desert."

"Oh really? Justin, I'll have them blow it up. If I have one of my men poking around and there are explosives in it, they could get hurt. That all right with you?"

"Thanks, Manny."

"Justin, you better hurry. That chopper is heading to town."

Justin rode the chopper back to where his squad car was. He made a call to his office and reported in. Justin learned that Mr. Jack Passmore was in town, and he had Nicholas Lockaby, the head of security of his company, with him.

"Okay, I'll be there in half an hour," said Justin. He just wanted to go home and drink a beer. *This is the worst part of the job,* Justin thought, going back to his office and facing a grieving father who would want some answers. This father might be upset and angry. Justin called Manny to get some instructions on how much he should tell Mr. Passmore.

Justin walked in his office and faced two men. The younger man was dressed slick, and Justin took him for the security. Justin turned to the older man and could see the hurt in his eyes.

"Mr. Passmore, I'm Sheriff Justin Smith."

"Sheriff, what can you tell me about my boys?"

"The state has taken over the case. They are better equipped to handle cases like this. We here are local cops. Captain Manuel Mendez of the state police will be in charge."

"I want an American in charge. You take over, Sheriff. I don't want no beaner handling this."

Justin looked up at Mr. Passmore and checked him out from head to toe. Passmore was well-dressed and in his forties. He had blue eyes and sandy hair.

"This 'beaner' will find out more in one day than I could in a week. He is a good man. He did authorize me to tell you that two bodies were found in the desert, and they are waiting for positive identification."

Officer Jones walked into Justin's office and handed him a paper. Justin looked it over.

"Mr. Passmore, you are requested to go to St. Pedro's Hospital. Do you need a ride?"

"No thank you, Sheriff. Nicholas will drive me."

*   *   *

Justin pulled into his home driveway. He sat in his car for thirty seconds before he got out. He slowly walked to his house and went inside.

"Hi, honey. Rough day?" asked Shirley.

"Shirley, I am so tired," Justin said as he put his arms around her and gave her a kiss.

"Wow, you must have had a real humdinger of a day. You need a shower. Why don't you take one and I'll fix you something to eat?"

"Sorry, honey, I've been out in the desert. I must stink."

"Nothing a shower won't cure. Now get going."

Two hours later, Justin was relaxing on the couch, watching television. A car pulled into the driveway, and Justin heard a car door slam. He got up and walked to the door. Justin opened it just as Manny was getting ready to knock.

"Manny, come in. Is this a social call or business?"

"Business, Justin," said Manny, still in his uniform.

"Come on in. I'll shut this crap on the tube off. We can sit here in the living room."

"Can we talk?" asked Manny. He was forty, and that day's heat wiped him out.

Shirley walked into the room.

"I'll get lost," Shirley said.

"Wait a minute. Shirley, this is Captain Manuel Mendez of the state police. Manny, this is my wife, Shirley."

"Good to meet you, Mrs. Smith."

"Good to meet you, Captain. Please call me Shirley. Would you like something cool to drink?"

"I'd like a beer, but I'm still on duty. No thanks. I'm fine."

"Okay, I'll be upstairs."

"Justin, as you know, the two young men we found today were the Passmore brothers. All evidence says the younger one beat his older brother to death and then wacked himself in the head several times before running off into the desert."

"Some kind of a fight, you think?"

"It appears that way. I don't have a motive, and when I try to talk with Mr. Passmore, he strikes out in anger. He wants an investigation and me off the case."

"And you have no background on the boys to know how they got along."

"I have no family history on the boys. The father is a big wheel at this chemical research company in Austin, Texas. But that is it. I was hoping to talk with the person who gave you the tip. Oh, by the way, I had the Range Rover blown up."

"Thanks, Manny. Could they tell if there were explosives in the Range Rover?"

"No, sorry, Justin."

"Damn. So Mr. Passmore wants a murder investigation?"

"Yes. He says his boys would not kill anyone. Can I talk with your tipster?"

Justin let out a long sigh. He then stood up and walked to the window.

"The person is one of Johnny Ramirez's biker friends. I told them I would keep it between us. The reason they reported it is because they did not want to have the law on them for it."

"Justin, let's find out all he knows and try to keep them out of it. That Passmore and his bulldog, Lockaby, will be looking for someone to blame."

"Let's try to keep it between us."

"I don't know if I can, Justin. I will try."

Justin got up and went into another room. He made a phone call and returned to where Manny was waiting.

"I made a phone call to someone who is going to try to set up a meeting with Johnny and his gang."

Manny got up and walked out to his car with Justin right behind him.

"I'll be in touch. As soon as I hear something, I'll let you know."

"Okay, Justin."

Shirley came out the door. "Phone call, Justin. It's Fruitcake."

"Wait a minute, Manny," Justin ran into the house.

Two minutes later, Justin came back.

"Ready to go right now?" asked Justin.

"Not really. I want to go home. Fruitcake, huh? Where are we going?"

"The corner of Fanner and Halsey Road. Don't ask."

"Out in the middle of nowhere, where you can see someone coming for miles."

"I think that is the idea. You can see a long way from all directions. Let's take my wife's car. It will be less official."

"Okay, Justin. Your wife won't mind?"

"She'll be okay. Let's go."

Manny and Justin arrived at the corners, and Justin got out and walked around the car.

"They are probably watching from somewhere," said Manny.

"I am sure they are. I can see one biker coming this way."

It was Johnny. He pulled up to the corners and dismounted his bike.

"Who is in the car?"

"Captain Mendez of the state police."

"Sheriff, I trusted you. Would you ask him to get out of the car?"

Manny got out of the car. Johnny walked over to Manny and held out his hand. Manny looked at Justin, and then Manny reluctantly gave his weapon to Johnny.

"That's what I like to see. Trust. I trust you, and you trust me. Okay, what do you want to know?'

"Everything you can tell us about what happened in the desert," said Manny.

"I think we told you all we knew."

"I know, and we want to believe you. The father of those two boys wants a murder investigation," Justin said. "Johnny, the preliminary investigation points to the younger brother striking the older brother with a tire iron and hitting himself with the tire iron. The father does not believe the forensic evidence and plans on using his money to mount a campaign for a murder investigation. That murder investigation could involve you or one of your friends. None of us want that when all the evidence tells us something else. If there is anything you can do to help us stop this before it gets started, that would benefit us all."

"Butch, one of my pals, was riding in the desert that day. He saw the kids' truck and was watching them. Butch says the younger one was acting drunk. They cranked up the radio, so he could not hear what they were saying."

Johnny handed Manny his weapon, and he continued, "Butch said they both acted a little odd. The younger one stripped and ran around in that hot sun. Butch said he did hear one of them say, 'Where's the can?' Whatever that meant. Then the younger one took a tire wrench and beat the bigger one to death. The kid whacked the truck a dozen times, hit himself in the head a few times, and ran off into the desert. Butch did not know the other kid was dead."

Justin looked at Manny to read Manny's face.

"What do you think, Manny?" asked Justin.

"Something made the younger one act like that."

"Drugs, too much sun?" asked Justin.

"We won't have the blood tests back for a week," Manny said. "We might need a statement. Butch is a witness to a murder."

"Yeah, well, good luck with that," said Johnny. "Come on. You know Butch was going to hijack that truck, but the kids came back. Who is going to believe him? You know guys like us. We tell little stories. This is the story Butch told me."

"Butch's story matched up with the evidence," Manny said.

"You done with me?" Johnny asks.

"Yes, thanks for your help. You have any questions, Justin?" asked Manny.

"No. Thanks, Johnny."

Johnny got on his bike and rode away.

"I like the drug angle," Justin said.

"Me too. I can't wait to get the toxicology report back. That should answer a few questions."

"Okay, let's go. You must be tired, Manny," said Justin.

"I sure am, Justin."

CHAPTER 2-3

THE AUTOPSY MEETING

Justin was sitting at his desk when Officer Jones knocked on Justin's door.

"Come in."

"Sheriff, Jack Passmore is here."

"Okay, Jonesy, send him in."

Jack Passmore and his shadow, Nicholas Lockaby, came into Justin office. There was no hello or pleasantries. Passmore went into his rage. Justin got up and closed the door. Justin remained standing.

"This is a cover-up. There is no way Eddie would kill Dwayne and then kill himself. Sheriff, I want you to look into this!" yelled Passmore.

"No need to yell, Mr. Passmore," said Justin in a calm voice. "As I understand, there is an autopsy being done, and blood tests are not back. You have to be patient, which may be hard to do. Besides, I do not have authority over the state police."

"I'll pay you money. You look into it and report back to me."

Justin had never had this happen before. He ran his fingers through his hair and opened the door.

"Goodbye, Mr. Passmore."

Passmore and his shadow left, and Justin sat down. He was expecting Jonesy or someone to pop their head in and ask if everything was okay. No one did.

Two days later, Justin was in his office when Officer Jones knocked on Justin's office door.

"Sheriff, Captain Mendez is on the phone."

"Thanks, Jonesy." Justin picked up the phone. "Hello, Manny, talk to me. Yes, I can meet you. Where? Okay, give me twenty minutes, goodbye."

Justin drove down to an abandoned parking lot where Manny was waiting. Justin drove around and pulled up beside Manny's car, facing the opposite direction.

"Hey, Manny. What is going on?"

"No drugs. No tumors. No nothing was found in their bodies."

Justin let out a long sigh. Manny took off his hat and rubbed his forehead.

"Well, what do you think?" asked Justin.

"I have to tell you something else. The doctor that did the younger brother's autopsy is dead. Right now, they are doing an autopsy on the doctor. But more carefully."

"Oh, what are you not telling me?"

"The doctor shot his wife and shot his home up, then he ran out into the desert, butt naked, and shot himself."

The two men sat in silence.

"Did you tell anyone about what Johnny told us?"

"No," answered Manny. "But you can see the similarities in the four deaths. Passmore went back to Austin with the bodies of his sons. Lockaby is staying here and nosing around."

"If it's not drugs, what do you think it is, Manny?"

"I don't know. Dr. Kramer is the head man at St. Pedro's, and he is a smart man. He will figure it out."

"Okay, Manny, keep me posted."

Three days later, Justin, at home, got a phone call from Manny. There was a meeting that Jack Passmore requested with Dr. Kramer. Manny wanted to know if Justin was interested in attending. Justin said yes.

Justin walked into St. Pedro's Hospital, where Manny was waiting.

"Hey, Justin, come on. We don't want to be late," said Manny.

They took the elevator to the third floor and found the small conference room where the meeting was being held.

"Sorry if we are late, Dr. Kramer," said Manny.

Dr. Kramer stood up and shook Manny's hand.

"Who do we have here?" asked Dr. Kramer.

"Sheriff Justin Smith, sir. It was in his jurisdiction that the first murder occurred."

"Hello, Dr. Kramer," said Justin.

"Hello, Sheriff. Come in and sit down." Dr. Kramer was a tall man in his sixties. He had bright-blue eyes that stood out beneath his bushy eyebrows. "I believe you know Mr. Lockaby. He is here on behalf of the Passmore family, who wants answers. And that is understandable. This is William and Elaine Wheeler. They are representing the Wheeler family, and I invited them. This gentleman to my right is Dr. Jamison from LA. Dr. Jamison is here by request of the Passmore family. He is regarded as an expert in brain trauma and all things related to the brain."

Dr. Jamison was a chubby man in his forties. He had dark-brown eyes with a full head of hair. Jamison was dressed in a suit, and Kramer wore a long white lab coat over his shirt and tie.

Kramer looked around the room.

"The sheriff and Captain Mendez are here because they have open murder cases that they want answers for, is that correct?"

"Yes, sir. We have no motive for the murders," explained Manny.

"Okay, let's get started. Edward Passmore will be referred to as A and Dr. Wheeler, the unfortunate doctor who did the autopsy on A, will be called B. A and B killed someone then killed themselves. This is what all the evidence points to. Am I correct, Captain Mendez?"

"Yes, sir."

"Why are we here? Because everyone wants answers, and no one believes the police reports. We did extensive autopsies on both men. No drugs or tumors were found. No trace of anything legal or illegal was found in either A or B. So this is a mystery. But Dr. Jamison did find something, and since he is the expert in these matters, I turn this meeting over to Dr. Jamison."

"Thank you, Dr. Kramer," said Dr. Jamison. "What I found was a small dark shadow on the edge of some brain tissue on A. It was also seen on B at the same location. The small shadows were not present in the murder victims. It should be noted. This may not be the cause of A's and B's actions. But the small shadow is abnormal. It is speculation and would take much further study to make an accurate diagnosis. I should also note that in all my studies, I have never seen anything like those small shadows. Now if B got them from A, then where did A get this unknown mystery? Is it from touch? Is it from something they breathed in? It is viral? Would their victims have died of this unknown cause? There are more unanswered questions. One thing is clear to me, and that is, considering the time frame, it is fast moving."

"Pardon me, Dr. Jamison. May I ask a question?" asked Lockaby. "Could the cause of this unknown death mystery still be out there?"

"Yes, of course. This, whatever it is, could be small. I would be very careful going through the belongings if it is a bug or something that carries this unknown danger. A was out in the desert and is the primary case. It could even be something from another world—some small germ that survived the ride in on a meteor. It could be something an alien left behind, if you believe in those things. We do not want any more deaths."

Manny jumped into the conversation, "We had forensics go through everything. They found nothing, but I would heed Dr. Jamison's words. If you do find anything, please report it. Call us or the hospital," said Manny.

"Any more questions?" asked Dr. Kramer.

"That's it? We still don't know much," said Mr. Wheeler.

"Sorry, Mr. Wheeler," said Dr. Kramer.

"Thanks," said Lockaby, and he got up and rushed out of the room.

Justin and Manny noticed the hasty exit.

"What was that all about?"

"I don't know, Manny, but it is curious," said Justin.

Nicholas Lockaby walked into his hotel room carrying a bag of things he had purchased at a hardware store. He laid a sheet of plastic on the floor. He reached in the bag and pulled out some rubber gloves and put them on. Lockaby went down to the truck and brought items from the truck into his hotel room. He laid them out on the sheet of plastic. Lockaby then reached into the hardware bag and put on a painter's mask and a plastic apron.

Lockaby started slowly going through each item on the plastic sheet. He was looking for anything that did not look right. Lockaby had no idea what it could be, but he had a hunch he would know if he saw it. He was aware that there may be nothing, but he wanted to be sure. Lockaby was also aware that whatever he was looking for could be so small that he might not be able to see it.

He had gone through everything but the backpacks. Lockaby slowly dumped the contents of the first backpack. The shiny silver can caught his eyes, and he reached in the hardware bag and pulled out a grabber with rubber tongs. He moved the silver can around and noticed its weight and its shape. It was like a beer can with no opening.

Lockaby studied the can, being careful not to touch it. He continued his search, and when Lockaby was through, it was the silver can that stood out as the thing that did not belong. Could this be the cause of the murders? Lockaby wrapped the can in layers of plastic then covered it with a pillowcase and placed it in a suitcase. Lockaby threw everything else in garbage bags, loaded the truck, and left for Austin, Texas.

CHAPTER 2-4

BACK IN AUSTIN

Nicholas Lockaby pulled into the parking lot at the campus of MPL Research Chemical Company. He picked up the pillowcase that held the silver can wrapped in plastic and went inside the building. Lockaby took the elevator to the third floor and went inside Jack Passmore's office. Passmore looked up, and Lockaby placed the package on the desk.

"Inside this pillow case is what I believe killed your sons," said Lockaby.

"What is it?" asked Passmore.

"It looks like a beer can, but it is something I have never seen before. It has some weight to it. It has no opening. I did not touch it with my bare hands, nor would I suggest anyone touch it. Unless they use thick rubber gloves. I think you should put some of your best research men on this and try to find out what it is."

"Is it dangerous?"

"Yes, sir."

"I did receive a report from Dr. Jamison, and it is hard to accept his theory. Okay, good job, Nicholas." Passmore went to his desktop phone and pushed a button. "Sharon, have Richard Stout report to my office."

"Is there anything else, Mr. Passmore?" asked Lockaby.

"No, take a few days off. If I need you, I have your number. Thanks, Nicholas."

Lockaby left Passmore's office, and thirty seconds later, Richard Stout walked in.

"Richard, have a seat. In this package, I have a mystery. I stress to you not to touch it with your bare hands. I believe it was found in the desert by my son, and it may have caused his death. I want you to find out what this can is about. I am told it looks like a beer can."

"You have not seen it, Jack?" asks Richard.

Richard Stout was a smart man. He was a middle-aged health nut and was a dedicated-to-his-work type of man. Richard had brown eyes, a full head of hair, and perfect teeth.

"No, Richard, I have not. When you get it unwrapped and in a safe place, then I will look at it. This is very important to me. And Richard, be careful and safe."

"How dangerous it is?"

"I don't know. It could be very dangerous."

Richard left Passmore's office with the package under his arms. He took it down to the first floor, where his personal lab room was. Richard set it on the table and put on some rubber gloves and a face shield. He opened the pillowcase and set the plastic-wrapped object on the table. Using his pocketknife, he cut open the plastic wrappings. With the rubber gloves firmly on his hands, he set the silver can up like a beer can. After examining it, he took all the plastic and the pillowcase and placed them in the trash. The phone rang in his office, and Richard went to answer it. When Richard came back, one of his coworkers was looking at the silver can.

"Stay away from that, Bob," Richard said in a firm voice. "You didn't touch it, did you?"

Robert Chambers, a twenty-five-year-old new employee, stood there, with guilt written all over his face.

"No, sir. Well, maybe I did just a little."

"If you did, Bob, go wash your hands and disinfect them. Do not tell anyone. This can may be dangerous. Go wash your hands."

Bob stood there and then, like a bolt of lightning, hurried out the room. Richard did not know what to do. He had to secure the can. He found a cabinet and locked the silver can in it. Richard then went to the men's room, where Bob was washing his hands.

"How do you feel, Bob?"

"I'm sorry, Mr. Stout."

"How do you feel, Bob?"

Bob started laughing. "I feel pretty good."

"Go to my office and stay there."

Richard went to Passmore's office and walked right by Passmore's secretary. Passmore was on the phone and said, "I'll call you back," and hung up the phone.

"Jack, we may have a problem. Bob Chambers touched the can."

"Where is he at right now?"

"I told him to go to my office," said Richard.

"Okay, let's go see him."

The two men went down to Richard's office. Bob was not there. The two men went to the front desk.

"Have you seen Bob Chambers?" Passmore asked the receptionist.

"Yes, sir. He just left."

"How did he act?" asked Richard.

"Happy. He was singing and had a bounce in his step."

"I'd better call Nicholas," said Passmore. "Is the project secure, Richard?"

"Yes, Jack, it is."

"Good, I'll talk to you later."

The next morning at MPL, there was sad news going through the building. Robert Chambers had wrecked his car and had burned up in the fire. On the third floor, there was a meeting with Jack Passmore, Richard Stout, and Nicholas Lockaby.

"We do not know if that is why he crashed his car. We do not know all the facts," reasoned Passmore.

"I think we should notify someone," said Richard.

"There is no proof of anything. No wrongdoing on MPL's part. No one needs to know our suspicions. Mr. Stout, you said you went to answer your phone, and when you came back, Bob was looking at the can. Is that right?" asked Lockaby.

"He touched it. I know he did. When I told him to wash his hands if he touched it. He almost ran to the men's room. I do not know how much of it he touched."

"That does not prove it killed him. I say we keep it between us," said Lockaby.

"Lockaby is right. We must be more careful. Agreed?" said Passmore.

"Agreed," said Richard.

Nicholas Lockaby nodded, and the cover-up began.

Richard Stout studied the silver can, but there was only so much he could do. He did not dare to cut it open. He was not sure he could cut it open. He weighted the can and measured the heat coming from the can. After two days of secret examination, he had nothing. Richard went to Passmore to ask for help.

"Jack, I need more ideas. People that can think outside the box."

"Well, Richard. You know there are rumors going around. Other workers know something is up. Your doors are locked, and people want to know. Who do you have in mind?"

"Ray Philips and Sam Dyson. Maybe Sara Conway."

"You sure about this?"

"Yes."

"I will confer with Nicholas and get back to you."

Richard was in his office, looking at his data. Someone knocked on his door. It was Lockaby.

"Mr. Passmore says you need help."

Richard did not like Lockaby, but he did accept Lockaby's authority. Richard also thought they should have gone to the authorities about Bob Chambers.

"I sure do. I took this can's temperature and measured the energy it's giving off. I do not know what else to do. I spend more time thinking about what to do than doing anything. These other people may have an idea that could open this up."

"What was the temperature?"

"Ninety-eight point six."

"Interesting."

Lockaby left and returned in twenty minutes with Ray and Sam. When they were all in Richard's secret lab, Lockaby had a document for them to sign. They started reading it, when there was a knock on the door. Lockaby let Sara in the room and locked the door. He gave a copy of the document to Sara.

"As you can see, we want to keep this a secret. You must agree and sign this document. It is mandatory if you wish to stay on this secret project. If not, please leave now." Lockaby looked at the three people.

"How dangerous is this?" asked Sara.

"We are not sure," Lockaby answered. "That is what you are here for, to tell us."

"Where did it come from?" asked Ray.

"It was found in the desert, in Arizona," Lockaby answered.

"Can we see it?" asked Sara.

"Only if you stay on this project," answered Lockaby.

"Did this have anything to do with Bob's death?" asked Ray.

"We don't think so," lied Lockaby.

Richard turned and walked away.

"What do you say, Sam?" asked Sara.

"Richard has been working on it for a few days, and he looks well. I trust Richard, so I'm in."

"Thanks, Sam. Richard, you hear that Sam is in?" asked Lockaby.

Richard walked back in where the others were and shook Sam's hand.

"Thanks, Sam," said Richard.

"I'm in. I'll sign the paper," said Ray.

"Against my better judgement, I'm in. I'll sign," said Sara.

After everyone signed, Lockaby took the documents and left the room. The others followed Richard into the lab, and he showed them the silver can.

"So this is the bad boy?" said Ray. Ray was tall and solid. He lifted weights and thought of himself as a bodybuilder. Ray was a little stubborn but knew his job.

"Looks like a beer can," said Sam. Sam was quiet and thoughtful. When he had an idea, it was always a good one.

"Why can't we touch it?" asked Sara. Sara was in her forties, a touch overweight but still a good-looking woman. She was smart and respected. The fact that she was a woman working for men was the only thing holding her back.

They looked at the silver can.

"To be safe, Sara. This is what I know," Richard began. "It weighs two pounds and has a constant temperature of ninety-eight point six."

"That is interesting," said Ray.

"There are no visible seams, and I do not know what kind of metal it is made of. I think cutting into the can could be risky because there is something radiating from the can. I don't know how to measure it. It could be dangerous."

"The top reminds me of a D-cell battery. How and who made it would be helpful," said Sam.

"Where was it found?" asked Sara.

"The Arizona desert," answered Richard.

"What if it was made somewhere else?" asked Sara.

"Like where? Russia? China?" asked Sam.

"Think bigger," answered Sara.

"Outer space," said Sam.

"I thought of that but was afraid to say it," said Richard. "I did not want others thinking I'm crazy."

"You are not crazy, Richard. I think Sara is right," said Sam.

"Another thing I found is that plastic is a barrier against the emissions from the can," said Richard.

"Let me see," said Ray. He put on one heavy rubber glove and reached out toward the can. "I don't feel anything. Let me try putting this thinner plastic between my bare hand and the can. Oops! I touched the can."

CHAPTER 2-5

THE COVER-UP

"I bumped it," said Ray.

Sara, Sam, and Richard all backed away from Ray.

"I don't feel anything. I don't feel any different," said Ray. "Are you sure touching the can is unsafe?"

"It was a precaution," said Richard.

Ray took the can in his bare hands. He smiled and started laughing.

"How do you feel, Ray?" asked Richard.

"I feel good, sort of warm all over."

"Put the can down, Ray," said Richard.

"Why? It feels good in my hand," Ray laughed.

"He is reacting to whatever this can is radiating. Richard, what do you know that you are not telling us?" asked Sara.

"I better call Lockaby," Richard said, avoiding Sara's question.

Sam and Sara watched Ray as Richard went in his office and called Lockaby. Ray seemed happy and kept breaking out in laughter.

"Lockaby's on his way," Richard said as he reentered the lab. "How are you feeling, Ray?"

"Good," said Ray. "I feel like dancing. Come on, Sara, want to dance?"

"There is no music, Ray," said Sara. Then Sara looked at Sam and Richard. "This is fast-moving. We need to secure Ray."

"What do you want to do, Sara? Lock him up?" asked Sam.

"You are not locking me up," said Ray. He grabbed the can and started chasing Sam and Sara. Sam started yelling, and Sara was screaming. Ray was trying to touch them with the can. Sara ran out of the lab and down the hall, followed by Ray. Sam was close behind Ray in his attempt to save Sara. Sam tackled Ray, and Ray pushed Sam aside. Ray stood up and struck Sam in the head with the can. Sam stumbled into an empty room and died. Sara found a place to hide in a janitor's closet.

Richard sat in his office and picked up the phone. Lockaby came in the office.

"Put down the phone, Richard," said Lockaby. "What happened?"

"Ray touched the can and started laughing and acting funny. I'm calling the police."

"Where is the can?"

"Ray ran down the hall with it."

Lockaby looked at his watch. It was almost quitting time. Another ten minutes and people would be leaving for home. Lockaby pulled out a gun and pointed it at Richard.

"No phone calls. Come with me," said Lockaby.

Ray had gone into a small lab where a man and woman were getting ready to go home.

"Hey, feel this can before you go. It is different."

The man and woman both felt the can, and soon they were all laughing.

Lockaby and Richard walked slowly down the hall. The building was almost empty now. Richard pushed open an unlatched door. Sam lay on the floor.

"Stay there," commanded Lockaby. Lockaby checked out Sam. "Sam's dead."

Lockaby motioned for Richard to move down the hall. Richard walked slowly until he came to a small lab where he heard laughter.

"Talk to him," Lockaby told Richard.

"Ray, you in there?"

"Yes, we are having a party. Richard, is that you?"

"Yes, who is in there with you?"

"Come in and see. Join the party."

Lockaby whispered to Richard, "See if you can get him to come out."

"Ray, come out to the hallway," said Richard.

"No. You come in."

There was the sound of laughter coming from the room. Lockaby decided to wait it out, but after an hour, he felt he had to force the situation.

"Richard, go in there and let me know what's going on."

"No."

"Get in there, or I'll shoot you."

Just then, Sara came out of the closet where she had been hiding. This startled Lockaby. He turned and fired one shot. Lockaby quickly turned his gun back on Richard. Sara lay motionless in the hall.

"What was that? Tell me, Richard. Was it that skunk Lockaby?" yelled Ray.

"He shot Sara."

Lockaby was standing to the left of the door where Ray and his two companions were. Lockaby was leaning against the wall nearest the door. Ray's fist came through the wall and almost grabbed Lockaby. Lockaby looked in amazement at the hole Ray's fist made.

"Did you see that? It's the can. It's the power in that silver can, isn't it?" asked Lockaby.

"Could be," answered Richard.

"This is amazing. This is what you should have been running tests on. You call yourself a scientist? You need to figure a safe way to use the power in the can."

"How are you going to do that, Lockaby? Ask for volunteers? How many people would have to die before we find the solution?"

"You would start out with rats."

"Well, Lockaby, this world does not need a species of super rats."

"You keep them contained."

"Yeah, that has worked well for us, hasn't it?"

Ray rammed his fist through the wall again, just barely missing Lockaby. Lockaby pulled out another gun. Lockaby shot Richard with the same gun he shot Sara with. Richard fell limp on the hall floor. Ray came flying out the door and into the hall. Using the second gun, Lockaby shot Ray five times. Ray fell to the floor, and the silver can rolled to within a foot of Richard's still body.

Lockaby walked in the room and, using the gun that he had shot Richard and Sara with, shot the two remaining witnesses. Lockaby then came back to the hallway where Ray's body lay. Using a handkerchief, Lockaby wiped the gun he had killed Sara and Richard with. Then Lockaby knelt by Ray's body. He placed the gun on the floor and put on a pair of rubber gloves he had in his pocket. Lockaby then lifted Ray's hand and pressed the gun against Ray's fingertips.

Lockaby then stood up and took off the rubber gloves and carelessly tossed them over by the can. He then got out his cell phone and tried to call Jack Passmore. Lockaby could not get a signal, so he went down the hall and entered an office and made two calls. The first was to Passmore; the second was to the police.

Lockaby went back into the hallway and started walking to recover the silver can. He stopped dead in his tracks. Richard was gone, and so were the rubber gloves and the silver can. Lockaby heard a car start and drive away.

The police sirens brought Lockaby's mind into focus. He had to get his story straight. Lockaby told the police that Ray went crazy and killed Sara, Sam, and the two workers in the room. Lockaby told the police he had to shoot Ray. He could not explain the holes in the wall. Lockaby decided to not mention anything about Richard and the silver can. After the police were done with Lockaby, Lockaby motioned to Jack Passmore. They went outside, where they could talk. Lockaby filled Passmore in on the truth, not what he told the police.

"We have to get that can back," Lockaby told Passmore. "I saw the power of that can, and I can see the possibilities if we can learn to control that power."

"I do not know about all this. We must cover all this up. Right now, this is a mess—one big stinking mess. We do not know where Richard or the can is. You better find him and make sure he is dead. Plus, find that silver can and bring it here."

"Mr. Passmore, I am sure Richard is dead or dying. I will find him or his body, and that is where the can will be."

"You better find it, Nicholas."

Richard had driven north to Oklahoma City. He was weak from the loss of blood. He pulled over a few times to rest. Richard had it in his mind to somehow destroy the can or hide it where it would never be found. He was in such bad shape that he was hallucinating. Richard kept seeing Lockaby and was sure Lockaby was following him. Richard did not know where he was when he pulled his car over to rest. *I'll bury it here. I'll take it out in the woods and bury it. I need a shovel,* Richard thought.

Richard still had the rubber gloves on. He picked up the can and got out of the car. "Maybe I have something in the trunk I can dig with," Richard said, talking to himself. Richard saw headlights and knew it had to be Lockaby. He threw the can into the woods and got back in his car. Richard then sped down the road.

The next day, around noon, Jack Passmore received a phone call from Lockaby.

"Mr. Passmore, Richard has an ex-wife and a son in Springfield, Missouri. I am thinking he might go there. I have to check on an auto accident. It's been on the news. Early this morning, a car ran head-on into a semitruck on Route 44. The body was burned beyond recognition. I have a hunch it could be Richard."

"He got that far?"

"Yes, sir. It is ten hours by car. I am going to try to find the silver can. I am sure fire can't destroy it."

"How can you be so sure?"

"I just am, sir."

"The police are going to wonder why one of our employees was up in Missouri after what happened here in Austin."

"I will be in touch. I have this under control. Relax, Mr. Passmore. I may have to call in some help."

"Okay, I'm depending on you, Nicholas. Goodbye."

Passmore hung up the phone and put his head in his hands. He wondered how things could have gotten so far out of control.

CHAPTER 2-6

HELLO, SHERIFF

Back in Tate County, Arizona, Sheriff Justin Smith sat in his living room. The phone rang.

"Hello, hey, Manny. How are you doing? No, I did not. Five people killed in an Austin chemical research company. Passmore's place of business. You think there is a connection? I do not know. What do you think? Yes, I remember what Dr. Jamison said. Yes, something about an alien that may have left something behind. No, I do not believe it. No, I do not believe in spacemen or Santa Claus. Okay, have a nice day. Goodbye, Manny."

Justin heard a knock on the door. He went and opened the door.

"Hello, Sheriff."

"Oh!" Justin was surprised. He turned his head and shouted over his shoulder, "Shirley, we have company."

Shirley came to the door and saw the one they once called a stranger.

"Oh lord. Dr. Dunn. How are you?" asked Shirley.

"Hello, Shirley."

"Please come in and sit down. So good to see you. How have you been?" asked Shirley.

"I have been well. I need some help and was hoping Justin could help me."

"Let's go and sit in the living room. Doc, you still have Fruitcake's clothes on," said Shirley.

"It's just human attire. How is Mr. Fruitcake?"

Shirley looked at Justin and saw that he was a little stunned.

"Justin, Doc asked how Fruitcake is doing."

"Sorry. I did not expect Dr. Dunn to be knocking on my door," answered Justin. "I believe Rick is doing fine."

Justin was quiet, not sure what to make of the alien's visit.

"Justin, Doc says he needs your help."

"Okay, sorry. What can I do for you, Dr. Dunn?"

"I am looking for something that we have lost. It is dangerous for humans to even touch. When we arrived back at my home, we took an inventory, and we realized one of our spoolas was missing. I looked at where we landed last time I was here. I saw the vehicle we drove there. You know it is all burned up. That, of course, alarmed me. I feared for your health and am so relieved you are well. I looked all over the site out there and did not find it."

"What is this thing you are looking for?

"It is a power source. Extremely dangerous and must be recovered."

"Oh boy," sighed Justin. "Does it make humans go crazy and kill?"

"What?" asked a surprised Shirley.

There was a pause, then the stranger from the desert said, "Yes."

"I am so ashamed. I have been holding back information. I did not want people to know that I had contact with Mr. Dunn and that I believed in spacemen."

"What is going on, honey?"

"Those two young men that died in the desert recently, I think they found it."

"Where is the spoola now?" asked Dr. Dunn.

"I don't know. It could be in Austin, Texas."

"Texas?" exclaimed Shirley.

"That is where the young men were from. They did autopsies, and an expert found something abnormal on one of their brain tissues. The doctor that performed the autopsy on one of the boys also died in a similar fashion. They go crazy and kill someone and then kill themselves."

"Justin, are you saying the doctor died from touching the body but not the spoola?" asked Dr. Dunn.

"Yes."

"That is new to me. I will have to report this. We are also learning. We knew if a human touched it, it would go directly into the bloodstream and to the brain. At first, they feel happy, and then they get a period of euphoria. Then their head aches, and then they die. Everyone who touches it dies. Now maybe everyone they touch also dies. Justin, please help me recover the spoola before anyone else dies."

"Too late, there were five deaths in Austin, and I think they are related to the deaths out here. I went with a fellow police officer to a briefing about the autopsies. This expert doctor said it was something he never saw before and said it could be something from outer space. I sat there and said nothing."

Shirley sat there, numb.

"Justin, they would not have believed you," said Dr. Dunn.

"Yeah, but . . ."

"Yeah but nothing. Put it behind you and help me find the spoola."

"It is a twelve-hour drive to Austin," said Justin.

"We will take my spaceship. We will get close and get dropped off and rent a car. You will have to drive. Can you afford this?"

"Have to. We are saving the world, aren't we?"

"That may be truer than you think, Justin."

"You okay with this, Shirley?" asked Justin.

"I want to go."

"No," Justin and Dr. Dunn said together.

"You two don't even have a plan. I have a plan."

"Okay, let's hear your plan. If it is good, you still have to get Dr. Dunn to agree."

"What do you say, Doc? Is your lie-detecting skill still work? Am I lying?"

"Shirley, you may be telling the truth, but I do not know how safe this is going to be," said Dr. Dunn.

"You'd risk my husband's life but not mine?"

"Okay, Shirley, what is your plan?" asks Dr. Dunn.

"Justin, put a uniform on Doc and take him everywhere you go. Ask your questions, and he can signal you if they are truthful. Plus, in a uniform, he can go almost anywhere without showing ID. No questions asked. Another thing is, we will take the laptop. And you know I am a lot better at finding out information than you are, Justin."

"Pack your bag, Shirley."

CHAPTER 2-7

AUSTIN, TEXAS

Everything went according to Shirley's plan. Dr. Dunn was wearing a Tate County police uniform as they drove through Austin. First stop was the Austin City Police Department. Justin and Dr. Dunn went in and asked to talk to the detective in charge of the murders at MPL research company. His name was Hadley. Justin and Dr. Dunn were directed to Hadley's office.

"Hello, Detective Hadley," Justin said. "I'm Sheriff Justin Smith from Tate County, Arizona. This is my deputy, Officer Dunn."

"Come in and sit down, Sheriff," Hadley said without getting up. He was in the middle of eating a big hoagie sandwich. He was a fat man, and his eyes never left the sandwich. "How can I help you, Sheriff?"

"We think that the murders in Arizona of the two Passmore brothers and the murders here at the chemical company are related."

"What makes you think so, Sheriff?"

"The similar way they died—someone going crazy and killing people."

"Those boys were probably on dope."

"The autopsies said they were clean."

"Well, these kids take all kinds of drugs, and some of them are untraceable. The killing at MPL is a clear-cut case of a disgruntled employee taking out his anger on the company."

"Could I see the police reports on the killings?" asked Justin.

"Sorry, Sheriff. This is still an open case, and we need to keep everything classified until the investigation is completed."

"Okay, thank you for your time, Detective Hadley."

"You are welcome, and have a nice trip back to Arizona."

Justin and Dr. Dunn went back to the rented car where Shirley was waiting.

"Hadley was no help. He lied about everything," said Justin.

"He sure did," said Dr. Dunn.

"What happened?' asked Shirley.

"Shirley, they are covering this up. That detective we talked to lied about everything. He was probably paid off by Passmore. Let's go see Passmore."

"Justin, let's call him and make an appointment. If Hadley is working for Passmore, then he most likely called Passmore and tipped him off about us. We do not know how far up the ladder Passmore's influence is."

"Good thinking, Shirley," said Justin.

"Let's break into Passmore office."

"Dr. Dunn, what are you up to?" asked Shirley.

"I want to search that building."

"How are we going to do that without being caught?" asked Justin.

"I have ways. You two stay in the car. Tonight, I'll go in and see what I can find out."

They waited till dark, and Dr. Dunn dressed in Fruitcake's old clothes. Then they left to break into Passmore's building. Dr. Dunn had no problem getting in, and he started on the ground floor. Dr. Dunn spotted the night janitor. He watched him for a while. The night janitor had a habit of talking to himself, and the things he was saying caught Dr. Dunn's attention.

"Yep, something ain't right in this building. I know. I can feel it," the janitor said, talking to himself.

"What is not right?" asked Dr. Dunn.

The janitor was startled and turned quickly to see who was there.

"Who are you? You are not supposed to be here."

"Relax, I'm Dr. Dunn, and I am here investigating the shooting and looking for what I call a spoola."

"Well, you don't look like an investigator. What is this all about?"

"This all started out in Arizona. What is your name? You could be a big help. The spoola looks like a silver beer can, but it is dangerous. And if you touch it, you die."

The janitor looked to be sixty years old. He was thin with baggy pants and suspenders. His hair was thin and gray.

"Well, there have been some strange things going on. How can I trust you?"

"The sheriff of Tate County, Arizona, is outside, waiting for me. Would you talk to him? He has his uniform on and all kinds of identification."

"I don't know."

"We went to the police station, but Detective Hadley was not too helpful. We are here to recover the spoola before anyone else dies. If I came to harm you, I would have done it by now. We need information. Please help us."

"Okay. I have seen Hadley. He is a fat, lazy cop. I overheard Mr. Passmore talking to him. They want to keep it quiet. As if you can keep five murders quiet."

"What's your name? Can I bring in my partner, Sheriff Justin Smith?"

"I have heard that name. Mr. Passmore often stays late and talks on the phone. My name is Steve. I hear a lot around here."

"Steve, Sheriff Smith is parked across the road. Come with me and tell your story to him."

"No, Mr. Dunn. I'll tell you everything I know or can remember, and then you better get out of here."

"Okay, Steve. Talk."

Dr. Dunn went back to the car where Justin and Shirley sat waiting.

"Did you find it?" asked Justin.

"No, but I had a long talk with the janitor. You know a man named Lockaby?"

"I sure do. You talked to the janitor?"

"Yes, I did. This man, Lockaby, he called Passmore. And Steve, the janitor, heard Passmore say that Lockaby was in Springfield, Missouri. Lockaby is looking for Richard Stout. Stout disappeared about the time of the shooting. Passmore said he was on vacation, but it was odd when Stout didn't come to any of the funerals. Rumor is that Stout ran off with this secret project they had been working on. I think that the secret project was the spoola."

"I think you are right. What do you want to do, Dr. Dunn?"

"Where the spoola is, there seems to be death," Dr. Dunn replied.

"Hey, guys, we need to monitor the news in Springfield and maybe the surrounding area," suggested Shirley.

"Good idea, honey," Justin said. "This is going to be like looking for a needle in a haystack. If someone has it and hides it, we may never find it. Let's go back home and regroup. I'll make some phone calls and see if we can get some help."

The three agreed, and they went back to Arizona.

PART THREE
TIMMY'S STORY

CHAPTER 3-1

FRED

It was early morning and still dark outside. Seventy-eight-year-old Fred McGraw sat on the edge of his bed. He reached over to the nightstand and felt around until he found his glasses. He placed them on his face then looked over to where his wife lay sleeping. Lylah and Fred married fifty-seven years ago.

Lylah was thin as a rail and looked like a child lying there in bed. Fred thought, *This is that one time I can look at her without Lylah having a cigarette in her mouth.* Fred got up and went in the bathroom. He relieved himself then took a long look in the mirror. His light-blue eyes that once sparkled now had faded to a flat gray.

Fred got dressed in his old-people clothes—black baggy pants and a plaid long-sleeve work shirt. He slipped his loafers on and went outside to his small garage, where his dog, Silly, was caged. Lylah would not allow the dog into the house.

Fred reached for the leash and let Silly out of the cage. Silly was all excited; he was eight months old and was full of energy. Silly was a medium-size white-and-brown dog of mixed variety. Fred grabbed a cloth bag with a long strap on it and put it over his shoulder. Fred then grabbed his grabber that he used to pick up beer and soda cans.

"You ready, Silly?" Fred said to his four-legged companion. "Okay, let's go."

Fred lived at the edge of town, and Fred and Silly walked a quarter of a mile away from the city to a side road. This side road had woods on both sides of it, and there were no homes for three miles. It had become a lover's lane and a party place for some of the young people growing up in town. To Fred, it was an excellent place to go and pick up cans and make a few dollars.

It was early fall, and the leaves had started to turn. Fred and Silly walked slowly down the road, looking for cans. Now that school had started, Fred would not find as many cans during the week, but the weekend would be more profitable. Fred had walked about a mile and a half when he spotted something shining in the woods. Silly and Fred wandered into the weeds and trees and found a plain silver can. Fred used his grabber and picked it up.

The can was silver with no markings on it. It was the size of a beer can, but there was no opening. Fred touched it and held it in his hand. It was warm and heavy. A smile appeared on Fred's face. Holding the can made him feel better, and he started to laugh.

Fred rubbed the can all over his body and then rubbed it on Silly. Fred began to whistle, and Silly began to bark. The two of them headed home, only at a much faster pace.

When the two reached home, Fred told Silly to sit. Silly sat on command. Silly had never obeyed before. Fred told Silly to stay and went into the house and returned with a bowl of dog food and water.

Fred walked by Silly and into the garage. He put the food and water down and called Silly. Silly came into the garage and looked at Fred.

"Eat," Fred commanded, and Silly did.

Fred sat in the garage, looking at and handling the can. Silly finished eating and came over to Fred. Fred started petting and rubbing the can all over Silly. The can rested on Fred's lap as he pet Silly. Fred began to laugh.

"Fred!" yelled Lylah. "Breakfast is ready."

Fred put the can on his workbench and walked to the house. He went into the kitchen, and Lylah was standing there with the coffee pot in one hand and a cigarette in her mouth. Fred could still see the beauty in Lylah's face and eyes.

Fred approached Lylah and took the cigarette out of her mouth and put it out in the sink. He then touched Lylah's face with both hands, and she set the coffee pot on the stove. Fred reached up with his right hand and pushed her hair back.

"No more smoking, Lylah," Fred says.

"Okay, Fred. You have that spark in your eyes."

"You bet I do."

Fred put his arms around Lylah and gave her a long, deep kiss.

Later that day, Fred walked out of his house and toward his garage. He heard the school bus as it stopped in front of his neighbor's house. Timmy got off the bus with his backpack of books. The bus pulled away, and Timmy walked toward his house.

Timmy was a skinny, shy fourteen-year-old boy with Coke-bottle glasses. His father had run off four years ago, and Timmy's mom, Stella, was working two jobs to keep the house and pay the bills. Fred liked Timmy, and he knew that Timmy's mom had a hard time.

"Timmy!" yelled Fred. "Come over here a minute."

Timmy waved to Fred and went over.

"Hello, Mr. McGraw."

"Timmy, how are you doing?"

"I'm fine. How are you and Mrs. McGraw?"

Fred laughed, grinned, and said, "Good, very good."

"You do look a little different," remarked Timmy. "Your eyes, they look happy."

Fred reached out to place his hand on Timmy's shoulder but suddenly pulled back. Fred thought to himself, *What if this is a bad thing? Maybe I should not touch the boy.*

"Timmy, if you want to make a few dollars, I'll have you mow my lawn."

"Oh, that would be great, Mr. McGraw. I sure could use a few dollars."

Fred reached into his rear hip pocket and pulled out his wallet. He pulled out a twenty and handed it to Timmy.

"You know where my mower is, and if you need anything else, ask."

"This is too much," Timmy said and tried to give the money back to Fred.

"No, you keep it. I hate to mow my lawn. You do it when you have time."

"Okay, Mr. McGraw, thanks. Thanks a lot."

Timmy ran to his house and went inside. Fred went in the garage and sat down, and Silly came over for some attention. Then the first pain came. It was an acute pain in Fred's head. Fred leaned forward and held his head in his hands. Silly then lay on the garage floor and whined.

Fred heard the lawn mower. It only increased the pain. Timmy was cutting the grass. Silly was whimpering in obvious pain. Fred stood up and went to the house. He had to see how Lylah was feeling. Fred found her on the kitchen floor. He picked her up and laid her on the bed in the downstairs bedroom. Fred sat with her, and finally, the sound of the lawn mower stopped.

Fred stood up and went to the garage. Silly lay motionless on the garage floor. Timmy went to the garage side door.

"Hi, Mr. McGraw. Is there anything else I can do for you?"

Fred looked at the silver can on his workbench.

"Yes, Timmy. I want you to do me a favor." Fred got up and placed the silver can in the cloth bag with the long strap. He then put it in a pail.

"Listen to me carefully. Do not touch what is in this bag. Take it out into the woods and bury it. Bury the pail and the bag also. Dig a deep hole and cover it up. Then you must forget where you buried it. Do you understand?"

"Yes, Mr. McGraw. Is something wrong?"

"Listen to me, boy. This can is something I found, and I now believe it is evil. Look at Silly. He is in pain."

Silly had begun to shake. Fred felt his hand begin to tremble.

"You must do this, Timmy. And don't tell anyone about this. Timmy, you must promise me you will do this, and do not touch it. And do not tell anyone. Promise me."

Timmy was now getting scared. Timmy looked at the pail that contained the bag with the silver can in it.

"Okay, Mr. McGraw, I'll do what you ask."

Timmy picked up the pail, and Fred handed Timmy a shovel.

"Do not bother bringing the shovel back, and do not come over here for a few days."

Timmy picked up the pail and the shovel and stood in the doorway. Fred went over to Timmy and placed his hand on Timmy's head and quickly pulled away.

Fred knew he should not have touched the boy.

"Go now and don't forget what I said."

"Okay, Mr. McGraw, I promise. I'll do as you ask."

Timmy went into the woods. He was cautious not to touch anything in the pail. Timmy dug a deep hole and placed the bucket and what it contained into the hole. He shoveled dirt over the container and then found some leaves and scattered them over the hole.

Timmy walked back to Fred's garage and placed Fred's shovel behind Fred's garage. Timmy then went home.

*   *   *

Bang! Timmy sat up in bed. He looked at the clock. One in the morning. Then moments later. *Bang! Bang!*

Timmy's mother burst into Timmy's room.

"Timmy, are you all right?"

"Yes, Mom, what is going on?"

"Honey, get dressed and come downstairs and stay in the house. I think that came from Fred's house. If I am not back in five minutes, call the police."

Stella ran toward Fred's house and saw that the door open and the light was on in Fred's garage. Stella took a quick look in the garage and returned to her home and called the police.

"What's going on, Mom?" asked Timmy.

"Quiet, Timmy," Stella dialed the police. "Hello, I want to report a shooting. Yes, 453 Dublin Road. I heard three shots. There is a dead dog in the garage."

Timmy ran out the door but stopped before he got to the garage. Timmy then had his first headache. He fell on the lawn, holding his head and passing out.

When Timmy woke up, an EMT was tending to him.

"You okay?" the EMT asked.

Timmy did not answer. A man in a suit came over and introduced himself.

"Timmy, my name is Detective Simon. As soon as you can, I need to ask you some questions." Detective Simon was a heavyset man in his fifties. "I have talked to your mom, Stella Williams. She is your mom, right?"

"Yes," Timmy replied.

"Your mom says you saw Fred earlier today. Is that right?"

"Yes, I mowed his lawn."

"Did you notice anything different or unusual?"

Timmy thought for a moment. He remembered what Mr. McGraw had asked him. "Do not tell anyone. The can is evil"—that was what Mr. McGraw had told him.

"No. What happened?"

Detective Simon breathed out a long sigh.

"I hate to have to inform you, but it appears Mr. McGraw shot his dog and his wife and then took his own life."

Timmy again felt that awful pain in his head. He covered his face the best he could. Timmy started to shake.

"Better get him to his mother," the detective said to the EMT.

Timmy was back in his bed. He had a severe headache. There were lights and noise from the McGraw house.

Stella knocked on the door and entered Timmy's room.

"How are you doing, Tim?"

"I have a headache that is killing me."

"I'll get you something. It will be all right. Rest is what you need."

"Thanks, Mom. I think I am going to be sick," Timmy up got quickly and ran to the bathroom.

CHAPTER 3-2

SCHOOL

Timmy spent three days in bed. He ran a fever and had long periods of headaches. Stella was going to take him to the hospital. But Timmy knew they could not afford it, so he told his mom he was feeling better.

"I'm going to school tomorrow."

"Detective Simon wants to talk with you when you are up to it."

"Oh, Mom, do I have to?"

"Honey, he is doing his job. He has called several times."

The phone rang. Stella picked it up.

"Hello. Yes, Detective Simon." She paused. "Timmy plans to go to school tomorrow. So if he can go to school, he can answer your questions." She paused again. Okay, I will tell him." Stella hung up the phone. "He is coming over, so get ready."

Timmy dressed for the first time in three days and got ready to be questioned.

In ten minutes, Detective Simon knocked on the door. Stella answered the door and let the detective in her home.

"Timmy, I have been waiting to talk with you."

"Why?"

"You, Timmy, are the last person to see Mr. McGraw alive. We are trying to understand why he would do such a thing."

"I came home from school, and he called me over to mow his lawn. I remember he was happy and gave me twenty dollars. I told him that was too much, but he said to keep it."

Detective Simon's phone rang. He pulled it out and answered it. After thirty seconds, Detective Simon hung up his phone and said, "I have to go. If you think of anything, call me." Then the detective left.

Timmy knew it had something to do with that silver can, but he had made a promise to Mr. McGraw. It was a promise Timmy wanted to keep.

The next day in school was odd because kids that never talked to him were coming up and saying how sorry they were about his neighbors. This much attention made Timmy uncomfortable.

Second-period science class had a surprise test. Mr. Everest, the science teacher, handed out the test sheets. When Mr. Everest got to Timmy, he said, "Just do the best you can."

Mr. Everest was a hard-nosed heavyset man. He always wore a white short-sleeve dress shirt with a bow tie.

Science was Timmy's hardest class, and Mr. Everest did not expect much from Timmy. Timmy looked down at the paper. Fill in the blanks; he had hoped for multiple choice. Timmy could not read the words, so he took off his Coke-bottle glasses. The words were now legible. He read the first question and knew the answer. Timmy put his glasses back on but kept lifting them to see the questions. Timmy could not believe he knew all the answers.

Timmy left the classroom feeling good about his answers. The rest of his day was routine except for kindness shown to him by the kids in school. Even the bullies backed off and gave Timmy some space.

The next morning at school was much different. Before classes began, Timmy was asked to report to the principal's office. When he walked in, Mr. Everest was there waiting. The principal, Mrs. Thomas, handed Timmy his science test from the day before.

"Timmy, do you know why you are here?" asked Principal Thomas.

"No."

"You have all the answers right. You even spelled all the answers right. Mr. Everest believes you cheated and is giving you a failing grade."

Mr. Everest spoke up. "Timmy is a poor student at best, and there is no way he could have aced this test. No one in class, except Timmy, got a perfect grade."

"What do you have to say, Timmy?" asked Principal Thomas.

Timmy was scared, but something told him to say nothing.

"Did you cheat? I am going to have to get your mother to come in. What do you have to say for yourself?" asked Principal Thomas.

"Oh no. Please don't ask my mom to come in. She cannot afford to miss work."

"Do you admit to cheating?" Mr. Everest demanded.

"Mr. Everest, would you please let me talk to Timmy alone."

Mr. Everest walked out of the room. There was silence in the room.

"Tell me, Timmy, what is going on. I know about the shooting, and I have no idea how it has affected you."

Timmy started to cry. "Please don't call my mom. She is working two jobs. She cannot afford to miss any work."

"What do you think we should do about this?"

"I'll take a failing grade and admit I cheated. Please do not make my mom miss work."

Principal Thomas was silent. She sat in her chair behind her big desk. Mrs. Thomas was an attractive woman in her forties that wore ugly pantsuits to hide what most of the boys thought was a beautiful body. She looked at the test paper.

"Do you and Mr. Everest get along? I feel some tension between you and Mr. Everest."

Timmy thought to himself, *I will not do this again. I will miss questions on purpose. It is that can. The silver can that Mr. McGraw told me to bury. He said it was evil. I did not touch it, but Mr. McGraw did place his hand on my head when I was standing in the doorway. Too much of the silver can kill you, but I was only exposed a little. The silver can made me sick, but it did not kill me.*

"Timmy, Timmy, Timmy!"

Principal Thomas was trying to get Timmy's attention.

"Yes, sorry, Principal Thomas. It has been a rough time for my mom and me."

Principal Thomas looked at Timmy and said, "What am supposed to do with you?"

Timmy sat with his head down.

"Okay, Timmy, you may go. I am not against you. I want all my students to do well. My door is open if you want to talk. If you did cheat, I'd like to know how you did it. It was a surprise test. You had no time to prepare. If you copied from others, you would have missed some because only you got all the answers right."

Timmy stood up and walked to the door. He turned and said, "I guessed at the answers. I was lucky, that is all." Then Timmy left the room.

Principal Thomas was alone and spoke out loud. "I do not think he cheated."

The rest of the day was typical for Timmy except gym class. The boys were playing basketball, and Timmy, who usually was known as clumsy, sat on the sidelines. The gym teacher, Coach Smith, sent Timmy in to play. Timmy ran out and, on the first play, stole the inbound pass and dribbled like a veteran ball player down the court and through the defense and made a fifteen-foot hook shot. Everyone in the gym froze, and the only sound was the basketball bouncing.

Coach Smith's whistle fell out of his mouth. Timmy said to himself, *No more of that stuff.* Timmy made sure he bobbled the ball and made as many mistakes as he could in the next few minutes. Coach Smith took Timmy out, and as Timmy walked by, Coach Smith said, "That one play was fantastic, Timmy, good going."

Timmy's bus stopped in front of his house. Timmy got off the bus and saw Detective Simon's car in the driveway. He went into his house, and Detective Simon was sitting with another man, and they were both talking to Stella.

"Mom, shouldn't you be at work?"

"Timmy, Detective Simon came to my workplace and brought me home. I want you to meet Agent Lockaby. He is from Washington."

"Hello Timmy," said Agent Lockaby.

"Hello," Timmy replied and exchanged nods with Detective Simon.

Agent Lockaby looked like he was at attention in the sitting position. He sat on the edge of the chair and straight as an arrow. Agent Lockaby was clean-shaven and as neat and polished as a man could be. He also looked like he could karate chop his way through a brick wall.

"Timmy, an autopsy was performed on Mr. McGraw. Now the man that performed that autopsy, John Withers, killed himself last night. His neighbors said he was acting strange the day before." Detective Simon paused for a moment then continued. "They said he was overly happy. He was singing and dancing in the nude in his apartment before he jumped out of his six-floor window."

"May I break in here?" agent Lockaby asked. "Nothing unusual was in Mr. McGraw's autopsy, but we have a suspicion that something happened in his life recently that caused him to act in the manner he did. We need your help in reconstructing the events leading up to his death."

"What can I do?" asked Timmy.

"Tell us his daily routine, his habits, things like that," answered Agent Lockaby.

Timmy had to be smart and think this through. His answers could somehow put him and his mom in jeopardy.

"Mr. McGraw walked his dog in the morning. He'd go away from town and down that side road," said Timmy.

Agent Lockaby was in charge now, "We found a grabber that people use to pick up things and a mess of different brands of beer and soda cans. Was Mr. McGraw in the habit of picking up cans?"

"Yes."

"Did he ever tell you about the cans or anything odd that he picked up?"

"No."

"We found a shovel with fresh dirt on it leaning against Mr. McGraw's garage."

"When I mowed his lawn, I picked up the shovel because it was in my way. I put it against the garage."

"Then your fingerprints would be on the handle?"

"Yes."

"Why didn't you put it in his garage?"

"I was going to later, but I forgot."

"Your mother says you were ill for a few days following your neighbor's death."

"Yes. I think I was overwhelmed. Mr. McGraw was like a father sometimes."

Agent Lockaby had eyes that penetrated. The agent's eyes looked at Timmy, trying to read Timmy's movements and gestures. Timmy looked down and decided not to move or show any emotion.

"I guess we are done here. Thank you, Timmy and Mrs. Williams. If we have any more questions, we will be in contact."

Agent Lockaby and Detective Simon left the house. Timmy watched them from the window until they drove away.

"What was that all about?"

"I don't know, Mom."

Timmy's eyesight had become so good that he did not need glasses. The problem was how to explain his much-improved vision. His schoolwork had improved, but Timmy made sure to make enough mistakes to avoid going to the principal's office. Mr. Everest watched Timmy like a hawk, waiting to catch him cheating.

Coach Smith watched Timmy in gym class, and now and then, Timmy would do something that would wow his classmates. Timmy knew he had to hold back, but now and then, he could not resist the temptation to show off.

The glasses problem had to be solved because wearing the Coke-bottle glasses were giving Timmy a headache. It was Wednesday night at the local minimart, and Timmy saw the glasses you could buy off the rack. He looked at the price. "Twenty dollars, damn," Timmy said to himself. He had already spent the twenty dollars Mr. McGraw had given to him.

Timmy started to walk out when he saw people buying lottery tickets. Timmy looked at the sign. The numbers were coming to him.

"How am I going to do this?" Timmy asked himself. You must be eighteen to buy a ticket. Timmy picked up a blank and filled it out. He then wadded it up and put it in his pocket. Timmy picked up another blank and filled it out, but this time he missed a few numbers.

Now I need someone to buy my ticket. Timmy looked around and did not see anyone he trusted and few he even knew. Timmy went outside, and he saw someone he knew. It was Jimmy Tee, a high school dropout and a bully. He was not alone. Jimmy had another dropout with him, Bobby Snow. Both were minor hoodlums, but Timmy thought, *I'll offer to split it with them.* Timmy reasoned he only needed twenty dollars for the glasses.

Timmy approached the two. Both were dressed in blue jeans and T-shirts and were smoking cigarettes. They could be rough, and Timmy knew he was taking a chance. Timmy stopped. He changed his mind and started walking away.

"Hey, Coke Bottles. How you doing?" Jimmy Tee had his arm around Timmy's neck, and there was no escape. "You know my buddy the Snowman, Bobby Snow."

"Yeah, how are you guys?" Timmy said in a shaky voice.

"Hey, that was some shooting up your way," Jimmy Tee said. Jimmy was doing all the talking.

"Yeah, a sad situation," Timmy said with Jimmy Tee's arm still around Timmy's neck. Timmy smelled the stench of Jimmy Tee's body. Jimmy was six feet tall, had a thin build, with long brown hair.

Timmy had to make his play.

"I was wondering, would you buy a lottery ticket for me? If I win, I'll split it with you guys."

"You got a hot number, playing a hunch, or what?"

"I have a feeling is all."

Jimmy Tee let go of Timmy. He looked at Bobby Snow. Bobby nodded yes.

"Okay, Coke Bottles. Your dollar and our dreams. One third for me. One third for the Snowman, and a few dollars for you."

"I need twenty dollars," Timmy said.

"You seem awful sure of this. Okay, give me the ticket and your dollar."

Jimmy Tee took the paper and the dollar and went inside and bought the ticket. Timmy stood outside alone with the Snowman. Timmy remembered the Snowman. Bobby Snow was in a fight at school that resulted in a suspension. He was a mean person to be around. Bobby had short blond hair and light-blue eyes. Bobby did not say much, but he had a pretty face and a reputation with girls.

Jimmy came out with the ticket.

"I'll hold on to the ticket," Jimmy Tee announced. "I have a feeling that you know how to pick the numbers. If this is a winner, I expect you to be here next week with winning numbers."

"I can't pick winning numbers every week."

"Your mom, Stella, she ain't bad for an older woman. I never could understand your old man running off as he did. You would not want your mom to get hurt. You understand what I'm saying?"

Timmy turned and started walking away.

"We know where you live."

Timmy heard them laughing, and he kept walking. He was in a bigger mess now than he had ever been. Mr. McGraw was right about the evil in the silver can.

CHAPTER 3-3

THE LOTTERY

The next day, Timmy came home from school and found Agent Lockaby sitting at the kitchen table, drinking coffee with Stella.

"Hi, honey, you remember Agent Lockaby?"

"Yes, Mom, I do. Hello, Agent Lockaby."

"Timmy, walk me out to my car. Okay?"

"Okay," Timmy said. "I didn't see your car."

"It's down the street. Let's take a walk."

The two walked out the front door and down the street.

"Timmy, I am going to be square with you. The government has many experiments going on, and some of them do not turn out as they should. We recently had one go bad, and the man involved stole the evidence and disappeared. He was found dead, much like Mr. McGraw. The reason we know this is because Mr. McGraw's body was taken to Washington and had a proper autopsy. The evidence is there. They both died, just like the man who did the autopsy on Mr. McGraw."

"Why are you telling me this? I do not know anything."

"Timmy, you are in a dangerous situation. I think you know more than you are telling. You could die, and those around you could die." There was a long pause. "Timmy, I have been to your school. Your grades have improved to the point that the teachers think you are cheating. Coach Smith says you have done things in gym class that amaze him, and then you go out of your way to goof up."

"So what? You can't prove anything."

"Timmy, I don't need to prove anything. I know you don't need those glasses. I believe you know about the missing experiment. Too much exposure and you die. Now, if what I believe is true, you have had the right amount of exposure. You are stronger. You are smarter than you were, and you are still alive."

"I don't know what you are talking about."

"Oh, Timmy. Don't be a fool. You need to tell me what you know. I'll give you a little more time. Then I'll have to come after you, and I won't be so polite."

Agent Lockaby got in his car and drove away. It was dark now, and Timmy walked back home. He went into his house.

"Everything okay, Timmy?" Stella asked.

"Yes, Mom."

"What did Agent Lockaby want?"

"Nothing, Mom."

"Timmy, you just lied to me twice. I'm your mother. I know something is wrong."

"I'm sorry, Mom. I must sort a few things out in my head, and then we will talk. You must trust me for the moment. Okay, Mom?"

Stella came over to Timmy and put her arms around him and hugged him.

"I love you, honey. You are a good son. Remember that. When you feel like talking, I will be here."

Timmy returned his mother's hug.

"Thanks, Mom."

Timmy went upstairs to his room and took out the junk in his pockets. He put them on the top of his dresser. Among the items was the paper he first filled out with the winning lottery numbers. Timmy lay across his bed with a freight train of thoughts running through his head.

Timmy heard the doorbell.

"Timmy, you have company!" Stella yelled from the foot of the stairs.

Timmy came out of his room and looked down the stairs. He could see Jimmy Tee and the Snowman.

"We have some money for you," Jimmy Tee said to Timmy. Then Jimmy and the Snowman started up the stairs.

"Wait a minute," Stella said forcefully.

Jimmy Tee and the Snowman stopped halfway up the stairs.

"Mom, it's okay. I'll explain later," Timmy said.

Stella paused and then said, "Okay, it's a school night, so don't be long."

"We won't be long, Mrs. Williams," said Jimmy Tee with a grin on his face.

The three boys went in Timmy's room and closed the door.

Timmy sat on the bed. Jimmy Tee looked around the room. Snowman stood by the door and pulled out his knife and started playing with it.

"Coke Bottles, you picked good numbers. Four hundred dollars, not bad. Not bad at all. How did you do it?" Jimmy Tee asked.

"Lucky, I guess."

"I do not believe you. How about you, Snowman? Do you believe Coke Bottles?"

"No."

"Snowman does not believe you either," Jimmy Tee said as he looked at the pictures on the wall and the junk Timmy had in the corner.

Timmy remembered the lottery paper. He had to distract Jimmy and get him away from the dresser before he saw the wadded-up lotto paper.

"I've been working on a system with numbers. Mostly guesswork. It is just a game I play," Timmy said, trying to divert Jimmy Tee's attention. It was too late. Jimmy Tee saw the paper and picked it up. He walked over to Timmy and pulled out fifty dollars.

"Here is fifty. The Snowman and I, we have expenses. Whatever your system is, we don't care. We want in."

Snowman slowly waved the knife back and forth. Then Jimmy Tee looked closer at the lottery paper that he picked up off Timmy's dresser.

Jimmy Lee looked at Timmy. "The numbers are almost the same. These are the winning numbers, aren't they?"

Timmy did not answer. How could things get any worse?

"We could have won millions."

Jimmy Tee puts his arm around Timmy's neck and squeezed Timmy.

"How come you changed the winning numbers? We all could have been rich."

The Snowman came over and looked at the lottery paper.

"Let me smack him."

"No, we must be nice to Coke Bottles because we are going into business with him. Don't you want to be partners with someone who can pick numbers?"

Timmy had to think fast. If that silver can was the reason he was smart, then he should be able to figure his way out of this.

"Okay, okay. We can be partners. I'll tell you my secret."

Timmy was still in the grip of Jimmy Tee.

"First, I want to know why you changed the numbers. The Snowman and I could be rich right now."

"I changed the numbers because I did not want a lot of attention. News people and things like that."

"Why?"

"I don't like a lot of attention. I thought it would be better to win a little at a time. You know, keep a low profile."

Jimmy Tee thought for a moment.

"You get a lawyer. He does all that legal stuff, and your name does not come out."

"I did not know you could do that."

"I still don't get it. Why keep a low profile? Unless you have something to hide. Do you have something to hide? Huh, Coke Bottles?"

"I told you I had a secret. If you want to be partners, there are some things I want. I can make us all rich. But I do not want to be bullied and threatened. I want my mom to be safe. I want to be safe."

"Sure, kid. I can understand that. The Snowman and I are not unreasonable. Are we, Snowman?"

Jimmy Tee looked at Snowman, and they both nodded to each other.

"Okay, Coke Bottles. Anything else?"

"I want to be called Tim. Not Coke Bottles."

They heard Stella coming up the stairs.

"Okay. Tim. We'll see you tomorrow after school. We will be here, waiting."

Stella knocked on Timmy's door.

"It's getting late. Tim, your friends better go now."

"We are leaving, Mrs. Williams. Goodbye, Tim. Let's hit the road, Snowman."

Jimmy Tee and the Snowman left. Stella followed them down the stairs and made sure the door was locked after they went.

Stella went upstairs and knocked on Tim's bedroom door.

"Timmy, we have to talk, now."

"Come in, Mom."

"I want to know what is going on. I work two jobs tomorrow, and I am not going to be able to sleep. I know something is very wrong. So you better talk to me, young man."

"I made a promise to Mr. McGraw. He told me not to tell anyone."

"Mr. McGraw would not want to see you in trouble. And right now, you are in a lot of trouble. Those two boys are hoodlums. You have a government man asking you questions. I have talked to Principal Thomas on the phone."

"Did she call you?"

"Yes, she did. She is concerned about you. I am concerned about you."

"I am sorry, Mom."

"Tim, I am not leaving this room until you tell me what is going on."

Tim looked at his mom and saw the worry in her eyes. He knew he had to tell her something.

"Mr. McGraw asked me to do something and not tell anyone. He made me promise not to tell anyone. What am I supposed to do, Mom?"

"This promise is causing a lot of pain and trouble. I think it's good that you want to keep this promise, but honey, there is a limit."

"Okay, tomorrow I'll talk to Agent Lockaby and tell him everything. Is that all right with you? And if Agent Lockaby says it is all right, I'll tell you everything. I don't know how many people should know. It may be a government secret."

"I guess that's fair. You talk to Agent Lockaby and get out of this trouble. Is this connected to those boys that were here?"

"Yes."

"I do not like those boys. They give me the creeps."

"I'll get rid of them, Mom. I promise. Now go to bed. You know how I am about promises."

"Okay, good night, son. I love you."

"I love you too, Mom."

CHAPTER 3-4

THE WOODS

The next day at school, Timmy went to see Principal Thomas. He had to wait in the outer office. Finally, Principal Thomas called Timmy into her office.

"What can I do for you, Timmy?"

"Thank you for seeing me, Principal Thomas. I have a favor to ask."

"If I can help you, I will."

"Do you have Agent Lockaby's phone number? I understand he talked with you."

"Yes, I did talk with him, but I don't have his number."

"Oh, I wanted to get a message to him. It is important."

"I can try to reach him. Detective Simon might have it."

Timmy thought about what he could do. He was counting on Agent Lockaby.

"It is important. I want Agent Lockaby to meet me at my house after school. I would do it myself, but I don't have a cell phone. And I don't know Agent Lockaby's number."

"A teenager without a cell phone. Imagine that."

"Money is tight, and my mom works hard."

"I will do what I can to relay your message to Agent Lockaby. Okay, Timmy?"

"Thanks, Principal Thomas."

Timmy went back to class with the hope that his troubles would soon be over. He was in his last peroid of the day when Timmy received a message to report to the principal's office. When Timmy walked into the Principal Thomas's office, she was standing and had a concerned look on her face. Timmy closed the door. He did not sit down.

"What is wrong?" Timmy asked, reading Principal Thomas's eyes.

"I could not reach Agent Lockaby, so I called every government agency I could think of, and no one knows him or has heard of him. So I tried to call Detective Simon, and he did not report to work this morning. And he is not answering his phone. I also tried to call your mom at work. They said a man came and took her home."

"Oh no."

"How much trouble are you in, Timmy?"

"Life and death," Timmy said as he covered his face with his hands.

Timmy sat down and slumped in the chair. Principal Thomas sat down but sat on the edge of her chair.

"How can I help?"

"I was exposed to something evil. First, it makes you happy, smart, and strong. Too much exposure kills you. That is why my neighbor died. I became sick, but I did not die. I must have had the right amount of exposure."

"That explains your grades. I had a feeling you did not cheat."

"Agent Lockaby, or whatever his name is, wants a small silver can. I assume he has my mom and Detective Simon is dead."

"Oh no. Can all this be true?"

Timmy could not trust anyone.

"I have to go. I have said too much."

Timmy got up and ran out the door. He did not have a plan. He was worried about his mother. Maybe Lockaby was legit. Why was Detective Simon missing?

Timmy walked home. He stood in front of his house. The door opened, and Lockaby stood in the doorway.

"Come in, Tim. Let's clear this up."

Timmy went in the house. Jimmy Tee and Snowman were inside, and so was Timmy's mom. They were all sitting in the living room. Timmy saw the fright on his mom's face.

"I'm sorry, Mom."

"I recruited your friends. I saw the show you put on down at the minimart."

"Yeah, Coke Bottles, we . . ."

"Shut up Jimmy. I want the silver can, and I want it now. Snowman is going to watch your mom while the rest of us get the can."

"Okay, don't hurt my mom. I buried it out back in the woods."

"Snowman, you watch the mom, and if Timmy doesn't produce the can, she is all yours. Okay, let's move. Timmy, you lead the way."

Timmy, Jimmy Tee, and Lockaby went out back, leaving Snowman and Stella in the house.

"I need a shovel," said Timmy.

"Where is it? Jimmy, you get it. I don't trust Timmy with anything in his hands."

Timmy pointed to the small shed behind his house. Jimmy went inside and returned with a shovel. Lockaby went to the side of the house and returned with a small duffel bag.

"Okay, Timmy, lead the way."

The three walked into the woods. Jimmy Tee followed Timmy with the shovel and Lockaby with his duffel bag. Timmy stopped and pointed to a spot on the ground.

"Dig, Jimmy," ordered Lockaby.

"Me? Make him dig," protested Jimmy.

"You don't get it, do you, Jimmy? A shovel in Timmy's hands is a weapon. Timmy doesn't know his capabilities. Now dig."

Jimmy started digging and complaining the whole time. The ground was soft, and Jimmy hit something. It was the buried pail. He dropped to his knees and dug with his hands as his moaning became laughter.

Timmy and Lockaby stared at each other. Lockaby dropped his duffel bag and pulled out a hand gun with a silencer on it.

"Is Detective Simon dead?" asked Timmy.

"He asked too many questions."

Jimmy Tee stood up, holding the silver can in his bare hands. He was laughing, and then he saw the gun.

"What are you going to do with that?" Jimmy asked.

There was a small pop from Lockaby's gun. Jimmy was dead, and his body fell to the ground. Lockaby turned the gun on Timmy.

"Who are you? And who do you work for?" asked Timmy.

Lockaby bent down and opened the duffel bag. He kept his eyes and the gun on Timmy. With his free hand, Lockaby tossed a grabber to Timmy and stood up.

"Pick up the can."

"Why don't you shoot me? You don't need me anymore."

"My employer wants you alive, but dead is fine with me. Now pick up the can with the grabbers and put it in the duffel bag. You will find some handcuffs in the bag. Put them on."

Lockaby put his gun away and then pulled out another weapon.

"This is a tranquilizer gun and will make my job easier."

"Your employer wants me alive, why?"

"Timmy, you are a rare person, the first one to live and benefit from exposure to the silver can. They will probe you and run tests. You will be a guinea pig. Now pick it up. And do not try anything, or I will shoot you and cuff you myself."

Timmy picked up the grabber. He squeezed the handle a few times as if to test it. Timmy walked over to where the silver can lay on the ground. Using the grabber, he slowly picked up the silver can.

All the time, Timmy's mind was thinking of ways to escape. He had an idea. As lame as it was, it was the only thing he could think of doing. Timmy held the grabber and felt a switch that locked the grip on the can. *If I throw the grabber and can at Lockaby, I can make a run for it. I need a diversion.* Timmy pretended to see something behind Lockaby.

"You are not fooling me with that old trick," Lockaby said as he lowers the tranquilizer gun for a moment.

Using the power and speed he had received from the silver can, Timmy threw the grabber with the silver can at Lockaby. Lockaby, in his haste to avoid the flying can and grabber, tripped over the duffel bag and shot himself in the leg with the tranquilizer gun.

Timmy had started to run, but when he saw Lockaby go down, Timmy stopped. He quickly ran back and picked up the shovel. Lockaby, still on the ground, spun around and pointed the gun at Timmy. Timmy swung the shovel and knocked the gun away. Lockaby was feeling the effects of the tranquilizer and slowly lay on the ground. Within a minute, Lockaby was out. Timmy found the cuffs and cuffed Lockaby's hands behind his back.

It started to rain. Timmy took the shovel and grabber with the silver can and went deeper into the woods. He dug a hole and buried the silver can. Timmy came back to where the two bodies lay on the ground.

The rain gave him an idea. Jimmy Tee had a T-shirt on with a gray hoodie. He took off Jimmy's shirt and hoodie and put them on. Timmy pulled the hood up over his head and leaned forward. He was not as tall as Jimmy Tee, but it was the only plan he had. Timmy started walking fast because of the rain.

Timmy walked up to his house and through the back door. The Snowman thought it was Jimmy Tee until it was too late. Timmy tackled the Snowman, and they wrestled on the floor. The Snowman had his knife, but Timmy had a grip on the forearm that held the knife.

Stella came from the kitchen with a frying pan and knocked the knife away.

"Call 911!" Timmy yelled to his mother.

The Snowman was tough and strong. Timmy was smaller but faster. Timmy thought the power from that silver can could help him prevail, but the Snowman had some tricks up his sleeve, and it was all Timmy could do to hang on.

"Hit him again with the pan," Timmy yelled.

Stella dropped the phone and came back, swinging the frying pan. She could not get a good swing at the Snowman because the two were all over the floor.

The front door flew open, and Coach Smith and Mr. Everest ran into the room. Coach Smith jumped into the fight and put a wrestling hold on the Snowman. Mr. Everest took the frying pan from Stella.

"Quit fighting, or I'll smack you," yelled Mr. Everest.

The Snowman gave up and stopped fighting. Timmy got up and ran to his mother.

"You all right, Mom?"

"Yes, are you, Timmy?'

"Yes, Mom, I am."

"I'm glad you two are all right," said Principal Thomas, who had entered the house behind Mr. Everest and Coach Smith.

The Snowman started to resist, but Coach Smith, the wrestling coach, had him in a locked hold. Mr. Everest came over by the Snowman with the frying pan.

"Where are the other two, Agent Lockaby and that creep with the long hair?" Stella asked.

They could hear police sirens.

"Excuse me, Mom, I have to do something," Timmy said and ran out the back door. He ran over to Mr. McGraw's house. The back door was unlocked, so Timmy went in and opened the refrigerator. He saw what he was looking for—a can of Coors beer in the silver can. Timmy wrapped it in a hand towel and ran out the door and into the woods.

CHAPTER 3-5

TIMMY TELLS HIS STORY

When Timmy came back to the house, the police were there and had Bobby Snow in custody. Stella was giving her statement. A man in a suit came over and introduced himself.

"Timmy?"

"Yes."

"I'm Detective Cameron. Can I get a statement from you?"

"Can I see some ID?"

The detective laughed.

"Yes. Yes, you can." The detective showed Timmy his badge, and they went inside Timmy's house.

Detective Cameron was a short, stocky man. He was almost entirely bald, had a full mustache, and wore wire-rimmed glasses. The detective appeared to be in his fifties.

Timmy sat at the kitchen table with the detective. The room was quiet. Stella, Principal Thomas, Coach Smith, Mr. Everest, and about six police officers were in the small house. Another officer came in and whispered to Detective Cameron and then left the room.

"There are two bodies out in the woods. What can you tell me about that?" the detective asked Timmy.

"Everything, but if I may, can I begin at the beginning?" Timmy asked.

"Yeah, sure. Go ahead, Timmy."

"Mr. McGraw found a silver can. He told me to bury it in the woods and not to touch it and not to tell anyone about it. Mr. McGraw said the can was evil, and I believe he was right. Mr. McGraw, as you know, killed himself and his wife. Detective Simon investigating the case introduced me to Agent Lockaby. We thought Agent Lockaby was a government agent, but he was not. He admitted to me he killed Detective Simon."

There were murmurs in the room.

"Lockaby is the man in handcuffs out back," added Timmy.

"Okay, hold it," Detective Cameron motioned to another man in a suit. They whispered, and then the man in the suit left. "Continue, please."

"Strange things did happen to me. I became smarter and more athletic. My eyesight improved. All because I was exposed to the silver can."

"Do you have proof of this?"

"Yes," Principal Thomas spoke up. "I am the principal at Timmy's school. Timmy's schoolwork improved so fast that we thought he was cheating. Sorry, Timmy."

"You say it's because of this silver can that Lockaby was seeking?"

"Yes, everyone who had contact with the silver can died. But I did not die. Lockaby was working for some private corporation that had an experiment go wrong. Lockaby was sent to find the can and clear up all the loose ends. He hired Jimmy Tee and Bobby Snow as a back-up. Lockaby killed Jimmy Tee. I saw it. Jimmy Tee is the other man out back."

"You want a break or a drink?" asked the detective.

"No, I am almost done. The three held my mom and threatened to harm her if I did not help them find the silver can."

"Excuse me, Timmy. How did they know you knew the location of this silver can?"

Timmy took a deep breath and wiggled around in his chair.

"I do not know for sure. I was the last one to see Mr. McGraw alive. Maybe because it was all Lockaby had to go on. I do not know, but he was right. I led Lockaby and Jimmy Tee into the woods where I buried the silver can. Mr. McGraw had wrapped it up and placed it in a pail. He had told me to bury it all and like I said he told me not to touch it. So I did what Mr. McGraw asked me to do."

"Tell me. What happened out in the woods?"

"Well, Detective, Jimmy was digging, and he hit the pail. Jimmy got down on his knees and pulled the pail from the ground, and then Lockaby shot him. Lockaby had a silencer on his gun. He then pulled out a tranquilizer gun. He had the intention of taking me alive so whoever hired him could study me. I made a quick move to run, and Lockaby stumbled over the duffel bag and shot himself in the leg. I waited for the tranquilizer to take effect and found the handcuffs Lockaby was going to use on me and put them on him. Then I came to the house and confronted Bobby Snow, and with the help of Coach Smith and Mr. Everest, we were able to subdue him and rescue my mom."

An officer came into the house and whispered into the detective's ear.

"Timmy. Did you at any time unwrap and look at what was wrapped up in the pail?"

"No. Mr. McGraw said, 'Do not touch it.' I did not even look at it. Detective, I think my mom and I are in danger because of the people that hired Lockaby."

The detective sat for a moment and played with his pen.

"I have a missing detective. I have a dead man. I have a man in custody that was impersonating a government agent. Timmy says this man went by the name of Lockaby and killed two people. I have another man in custody for kidnapping and holding someone against their will. I have a feeling the two in custody won't talk. But we will find out more when we get Lockaby's fingerprints. Now the part I find hard to believe is the silver can part. This magical silver can that has made Timmy smarter and stronger. This silver can that people want so bad that they are willing to kill for it. This silver can that will kill you from too much exposure. And Timmy believes that his mother and he are in danger because of this silver can. Do I have that right?"

"Yes, sir," Timmy answered.

"And the part about Lockaby stumbling and shooting himself is a little . . . lucky for you. If what you say is true."

Timmy looked at the detective and shrugged his shoulders.

"Sergeant Kelley, bring in here the bundle found in the woods."

A man in uniform brought in Mr. McGraw's bag with the long handle and placed it on the table. Timmy jumped up and backed away.

Using his pen, the detective unwrapped the bag. He then reached into the bag and pulled out a silver can. He placed the silver can on the table. When he removed his hand, everyone could see it was a can of Coors beer.

There was silence in the room.

"Is this the silver can?"

"He switched cans. Mr. McGraw, old Fred, he had me bury a fake can, or he followed me and later dug it up and switched cans."

Detective Cameron stood up. "Okay, ladies and gentlemen, let's get back to work. Pick up all the evidence. I want to thank everyone for their cooperation. If we need to talk with anyone, we will be in touch. I'll leave a squad car and two uniformed officers out front for tonight. Tomorrow, we will see what happens."

Everyone left, and Timmy and his mom were finally alone.

"What are we going to do, Timmy? I have missed a lot much work. I may not have a job to report to tomorrow. Detecive Cameron doesn't believe the silver can story."

"The detective must think it is a hoax or BS about the silver can. But he must wonder why people around this story are dying. I have a plan. Mom, we need to borrow a car. Maybe Principal Thomas will help us. We will make a trip to the minimart and buy a lotto ticket. Then we will need to find a good lawyer."

PART FOUR
LOU'S STORY

CHAPTER 4-1

THE DETECTIVE AND LILLY

Detective Cameron pulled his car into the Williamses' driveway. He sat in his car and took a long look at the For Sale sign in the front yard—Sandusky Realtors. *I'll call them,* the detective told himself. The detective had been calling Stella on the phone with no answer. First, he tried Stella's workplace, and they said she did not go to work. Then he tried her residence with no response.

The detective got out of his car and went to the house. He knocked on the door then looked through the windows. He saw the furniture was still there, but the pictures on the walls were gone.

Three days ago, there had been a murder in the woods out back. There were two men in custody, and the county prosecutor wanted to talk with Timmy, who was a witness to the murder and had information on a second possible murder.

Detective Cameron went back and sat in his car. It was a crisp fall day, and Detective Cameron's fifty-five-year-old body did not like the cold. He flexed his hands by opening and closing them several times. There was no pain like there had been earlier last week. Arthritis had been a problem for the detective but not now.

It's the can, he thought. Timmy had said the silver can was dangerous. That mysterious can was another reason he wanted to speak with the fourteen-year-old. Detective Cameron was a nonbeliever in the silver can, but he felt that there might be something to this can.

The detective saw a car in the driveway of the now-deceased Fred McGraw. He wondered if they knew anything about the Williamses. Timmy said Fred found the silver can, and it led to Fred killing his wife, his dog, and himself.

The detective flexed his hand again. He couldn't believe it. He never touched the can or saw it. All he did was reach into the bag where it was alleged to have been.

Detective Cameron got out of his car and knocked on Fred McGraw's house door. A woman about the detective's age opened the door.

"Sorry to disturb you, but . . . sorry again. I'm Detective Cameron with the Springfield City Police. I wanted to ask you a few questions."

"Please come in. Have a seat. Would you like a cup of coffee?"

"Oh no. Miss . . ."

"Turner, Mrs. Lilly Turner. I am the daughter of Fred and Lylah. I'm here to take care of things."

"Yes, I should not bother you. My condolences about your family. I wanted to talk with the Williams family, but they seemed to have vanished."

"Please sit down and have a cup of coffee, and I will tell you all I know."

"Well, okay, but I cannot stay long."

The detective sat at the kitchen table, and Lilly placed two mugs on the table and poured out the coffee. She opened the refrigerator to get some milk, and the detective was able to see the Coors beer in the fridge.

Lilly then sat down.

"I drink it black . . ."

"Call me Lilly. Lilith is my given name, but I always hated it. I drink my coffee with just a little cream. What would you like to know, Detective?"

"What can you tell me about anything that you may have observed from next door?"

They both sipped from the coffee mugs. The detective felt comfortable sitting with this woman. His wife had passed away five years ago from cancer. He had buried himself in his work and had not even thought about another woman till now.

"I arrived Saturday morning, and on Sunday morning, well, all day Sunday things were going on. A van pulled in, and they were putting things in the van. Not big things but small personal things. Clothes, boxes of pictures, I think. And then they left, and this morning a man stopped and put a For Sale sign in the front yard."

"Was anyone with the Williamses?"

"No, just Stella and the boy. My husband was killed in an automobile crash a few years ago. I am thinking of moving back here. I have a brother out in Ohio, and he told me to do whatever I want with the place." Lilly then leaned forward and looked into the detective's eyes. "I am telling you this because I think you are checking me out."

The detective looks away quickly. He was embarrassed.

"I'm a widower and have not dated or sought a woman's attentions since I lost my wife."

"Nor have I wanted a man since my husband passed. Sam was a great husband, and he left me financially comfortable. Not rich, but I won't starve for a good while."

They were quiet and drank their coffee. *It's that damn silver can,* Detective Cameron thought to himself.

"Could I take you to dinner sometime?" the detective asked.

"Why don't you come by tonight, about six, and I'll fix you dinner?"

"Okay, I'll be here."

"What would you like?"

"Anything is fine. I am not a fussy eater."

"Okay, peanut butter and jelly sandwiches will be served."

"Okay," the detective laughed.

"I have been sleeping in my parents' bed the last two nights, and when I get up in the morning, I have no aches or pains. I feel excellent except for a minor headache. I can smell or sense something in the bed or on the sheets. I guess you think I'm silly."

"No, I don't. Did you wash the sheets?"

"No, I should be ashamed, but I don't think I'll ever wash the sheets."

"Can I see the bed?"

Lilly laughed. "Can't wait till six?"

She did not wait for an answer. Lilly got up from the table and went to the downstairs bedroom, where she had been sleeping. Detective Cameron followed Lilly into the bedroom.

"Can I lay down?"

Lilly laughed even harder. "If you want to."

The detective lay on the bed. He was trying to feel what Lilly felt—the residue of someone who had touched the can.

"It might have more effect if you take off your clothes," Lilly said with a big smile on her face.

"I already feel foolish."

"What if I took my clothes off and lie there with you? What do you say, Detective?"

"Call me Lou."

*   *   *

Detective Cameron was back at his desk, making some notes. It was early afternoon, and he had to call Sandusky Realtors. He had to find out more about the location of Timmy and Stella.

Officer Bobbi Jackson carried a folder as she walked over to the detective's desk. She was in her thirties and still turning heads.

"You need an office, Lou. Go in there and tell the chief you want an office. You are a better detective than those other guys."

"Thanks, Bobbi. What do you have?"

"Surprise, surprise, Lockaby is his real name. Nicholas Lockaby, an FBI school dropout. He got into some gambling trouble, and well, you can read the rest."

Officer Jackson walked around the desk and put the folder in front of the detective.

"Lou, you reek of sex, and I know about sex."

Lou rolled his eyes and said nothing. The detective watched Bobbi as she walked away. He had to admit she was a looker, but sometimes she had a potty mouth. The detective's eyes left Bobbi and picked up Tom Wills walking right toward him. Tom Wills was out of the DA's office.

Lou stood up and said, "Hello, Tom."

"Hello, Lou." Tom was young and good-looking, eager to climb the ladder of success. "What do you have on the Jimmy Tee murder? Don't you have an office?"

"I have a witness. And my witness says Lockaby killed Detective Simon."

"We need him to come in and talk to us as soon as possible."

"Okay, Tom, I know the drill. My witness has expressed his concern that whoever Lockaby worked for is after him."

"What do you need?"

"Well, I'd like a small task force of maybe two people to help me get to the bottom of this. I think there is a lot here to unpack."

"I'll talk to the chief. Who do you want?"

"Sergeant Brian Kelley and Officer Bobbi Jackson for research."

"Okay, I am doing this because of Detective Simon. We need to take care of our own. You know what I mean. I'll see if I can get you an office."

Tom left as quickly as he came. Lou picked up the phone and called Sandusky.

"Hello, this is Detective Cameron. Yeah, the city police. Who is handling the Williamses' house on Dublin Road? No, I do not want to buy. Stop, stop, this is police business. Who talked to whom about putting the house on the market? Okay, thank you. Goodbye."

Bobbi came walking over.

"I heard you might get an office, Lou, and I heard you are heading a task force. What big case are we working on?"

"The Detective Simon case."

"Yeah, that is a big one. Must take care of our own."

"I just talked to Sandusky Realtors. Jacob Weinstein is representing his client in the sale of the Stella Williams house."

"Jacob Weinstein, the uppity lawyer?"

"Yes, where did the Williamses get the money to hire him?"

"Oh, oh, oh. I think I know. Someone hit the lottery Saturday night at Clark's grocery. Five point four million dollars, I heard. Could be Stella Williams. No one has come forward."

"Bobbi, you are going to be an asset to this team. Could you get Sergeant Brian Kelley? I need to talk with him."

"You got it, boss."

She left, and the detective looked at his watch. Three o'clock. He needed to have enough time to go home and get cleaned up and be back to Lilly's house by six. Bobbi came back to Lou's desk.

"He is on his way."

"Thanks, Bobbi. One of the first things I want you to do is try to find out who Lockaby was working for and then find out as much as you can about them."

"Got it, boss."

"And don't call me boss."

"Oh, come on, Lou. It makes me feel important. Here comes Kelley."

Sergeant Brian Kelley was in his late twenties and had moved up in rank fast. Some said it was because his father was a hero cop killed in action while stopping a holdup. Kelley's father had received some big awards posthumously. Brian Kelley was clean looking and quiet. Detective Cameron believed Kelley needed a chance to get out of his father's shadow.

"Sergeant, sit down."

Kelley sat in the only chair near the desk.

"How come you don't have an office?"

Detective Cameron looked at the floor. Then he looked up at Kelley.

"You want to work on this case?"

"What is this case?"

"You know Detective Simon is missing. That case, the Fred McGraw case, and the Williams case. I think they are all connected. I want you on my task force."

"You want me?"

"You were out there at the Williamses' house last Friday. How has your health been since then?"

"Good, excellent."

"Anything unusual?"

"Like what?"

Detective Cameron wondered if he had the right man. He looked around the room to see if anyone was watching. No one appeared to be interested. The detective leaned in a little, put his hand out, and opened and closed it.

"Last week, I could not do that without pain. Now my arthritis seems to have gone away. How about you?"

"Well, I was coming down with a cold on Thursday, but then it disappeared. I bowled with the guys on Saturday, and I bowled three games over two hundred. I'm a one forty bowler. To be honest, I don't even like bowling, but I like to hang out with the guys."

"Was there anyone else handling the sack that held the alleged silver can?"

"No, only me. You think it is this silver can the kid was talking about?"

"I do not want others knowing I believe in this can. They will think I am crazy for sure. Are you in?"

"Didn't the kid say too much exposure would kill you? We only touched something that touched it."

"We are going to solve the murder of Detective Simon. Then we have a few loose ends to clear up. You and I have seen and felt the power of this can."

"So I did not bowl that on my own? It was the silver can magic?"

"Yes, I think so. The silver can must be found and studied, but by good people."

"I'm in. So I did not bowl the two hundred games on my own?"

"No. I got to go. Tomorrow I'll fill you in. Do not mention the silver can to anyone."

"Okay. Crap, I thought I bowled excellently."

The detective got up and headed out the door. He had an appointment at six.

CHAPTER 4-2

THE BREAK-IN

Lou arrived at Lilly's house at six, all cleaned up from head to toe. He started to knock on the door when the door opened. Lilly was standing there in a long negligee and a big smile on her face.

"Come in, Detective. I was beginning to worry you weren't coming."

"It has been a busy day, and please call me Lou."

"Okay, Lou."

Lilly took Lou's hand and led him into the kitchen. Lou looked at the table dressed in a white tablecloth with candlelight, two plates, a loaf of bread, a jar of peanut butter, and a jar of jelly.

"Lilly, that looks . . . perfect."

"Guess what is for dessert."

"Lilly. How can you top this?"

"Come on, Lou. Where is your imagination?" Lilly stepped back and outstretched her arms and said, "Ta-da," in an extended musical tone.

It was almost midnight. Lilly and Lou were lying in bed, telling each other about their families. Lou was telling Lilly about his daughter.

"Janey is a pretty girl, but wild. She ran off with some damn guitar player, and I think they are in New Zealand. Did you hear that?"

"Hear what, Lou?"

Lou got out of bed and looked out the window toward the Williamses' house.

"Lilly, call 911. Someone is breaking into the Williamses' house."

Lou was getting dressed as fast as he could, and Lilly had 911 on the phone.

"Lilly, stay on the phone. I must get my gun. It is in my car."

"Be careful, Lou."

Lou's stocky body was not designed for crouching and sneaking, but the detective was nimble and quick. He went out the back door and squatted next to his car. The detective remembered that once he pushed the button to unlock his car's door, the lights would come on and tip off the people breaking in. He pushed the button, and the car lights came on. Lou opened the car door and retrieved his gun. The detective ran around to the back of the Williamses' house.

"POLICE. Hold it right there!" yelled Lou.

It was dark, but the detective could see two of them well enough to shoot if they tried anything. The police sirens warned them of their arrival. Lou heard a sound from the house. *There must be another one,* Lou thought, *I am going to be in the middle of this.* It was too late. The third man came running out the back door. The police were in the driveway and running toward the house.

Detective Cameron turned, and the third man, carrying a bag, ran into the detective. The detective and the third man wrestled on the ground. The first two crooks ran off into the darkness. Police lights were everywhere, and uniformed police officers broke up the wrestling match.

"I'm a cop!" yelled Lou. "I'm Detective Cameron."

"Okay. Sorry, Detective. Are you all right?" asked one of the uniformed officers.

"Yes, thanks."

"What were you doing here?" asked the officer.

"I was staking out the place."

"Staking out the place. Come on, Lou. I'll take it from here, Officer. Thanks." It was Bobbi.

"Lou, are you okay?" Lilly asked in a concerned voice.

Bobbi turned and looked at Lilly, who had found her way over to the Williamses' house in a night-robe.

"Staking out the place, huh, Lou? You been having sex again?"

Good thing it is dark, Lou thought as he rolled his eyes.

"Bobbi, this is Lilly. Lilly, this is Officer Bobbi Jackson. Bobbi is on my task force. Why are you here, Bobbi?"

"Well, boss, I was up late and heard the call and recognized the address."

"Hi, Bobbi. I am Fred McGraw's daughter, and I am the one who called 911."

Bobbi laughed, and the two women shook hands. Sergeant Kelley walked onto the crime scene.

"Hello, everyone. Okay, what can I do to help? I was called and told to report here."

"Sergeant, glad to have you here. There were three. Two ran off, and we have the third one in custody, I think. Now the third had a bag, and I am interested in finding out what is in that bag."

"Lilly, if Lou won't introduce you, then I will. Sergeant Kelley, this is Lilly. Lilly, this is Sergeant Kelley. He is on the task force with me."

Lilly and Sergeant Kelley exchanged greetings.

"Lilly, you better go back inside, and I'll stop and see you when this is over."

"Okay, Lou. It is a little chilly. I'll put on some coffee, and if anyone wants a cup of coffee or a peanut butter and jelly sandwich, stop over."

Lilly left, and Bobbi started laughing so hard she had to hold on to Kelley so she wouldn't fall. Kelley smiled but did not know the whole story.

"I'll get some gloves and look into the bag," Kelley said to the detective.

"Thanks, Sergeant," replied the detective.

"Burglars?" asked Bobbi.

"I don't think so. That kid, Timmy, said he was in danger."

Kelley came back and looked at the detective and said, "I am beginning to believe it. There was a stun gun, a tranquilizer gun, handcuffs, and ropes in that bag."

"Believe what?" Bobbi asked.

"They wanted to take Timmy alive," Lou answered.

"I think if I am on this task force, you two better fill me in because I think you know a lot more than I do. And who are they that want to take Timmy alive?"

"The company that hired Lockaby. They want Timmy alive."

"Well, boss, what have you got me into here?"

"Let's get all the evidence, and tomorrow, I'll brief everyone and bring you up to speed, Bobbi."

"Is this anything to do with the silver can rumors I have been hearing?"

"Bobbi, don't tell anyone. But yes. I do not have a shred of proof that the silver can even exists. If the can is as dangerous as that kid said it is, the right people better control it."

"Boss, you are beginning to scare me. You know about this, Sergeant Kelley?"

"Some."

"Okay, let's go home and get some rest, everybody."

"Hey, boss, you going to see the peanut butter and jelly lady?"

"Yes, Bobbi, I am."

"Do you think I could get some coffee and a peanut butter and jelly sandwich to go?"

CHAPTER 4-3

THE FACTS

The next morning, Detective Cameron walked into the police station and went to where his desk had been for years. The detective stood there for a moment and stared at the empty space.

Bobbi hooked her arm around Lou's, and then, with a big smile on her face, she said, "Want to see your office, Detective Cameron?"

Bobbi led the detective down the hall and to a small room where his desk sat. Two folding tables were set up. One of the tables had a computer on it.

"This one with the computer is mine. I think you and Kelley will get yours later. The chief wants you to have a meeting at ten and get everyone up to date on your investigation. I found out who Lockaby is or was working for, a company called MPL. Myers, Passmore, and Larkin, a chemical research company."

"Anything on the man we caught breaking in last night?"

"No, not yet, but he is a foreigner. He talks with a heavy accent. But from where we don't know because he does not say much. Kelley made a list of the contents of the bag the man had. The two that got away left some remarkable shoe prints that forensics are going over."

"Good job, Bobbi."

"Thanks, boss."

"Stop that."

"Stop what?"

"Calling me boss. Okay, I must go over these papers and get ready for this meeting. Where is Kelley?"

"There was an accident late last night on Route 44. A dark van with Texas plates got totaled by a semitruck. Two men dressed in black were pronounced dead at the scene. They had a gun and some other incriminating items. Sergeant Kelley went to check it out."

"Hell, I have some good help."

Detective Cameron got busy making notes and reading the backgrounds on Lockaby and the MPL company.

At five to ten, the detective's new office began to fill up. There was the detective, Bobbi, Tom Wills from the DA's office, Joe Spinner from forensics, the chief, and two of the chief's shadows all cramped into Lou's little office.

The detective was ready to begin when Sergeant Kelley opened the door and squeezed into the room. He handed a paper to Lou.

The detective with the wire-rimmed glasses and full mustache played with his pen while he read Kelley's paper. The room became quiet.

"We have a missing detective, Detective Simon. One of our own who may be dead. We have an eye witness, Timmy Williams, who saw Nicholas Lockaby, an FBI school dropout, shoot and kill Jimmy Tee, real name James Teeter. Our witness, Timmy Williams, also said Lockaby admitted to him that Lockaby killed Detective Simon. Our suspect, Nickolas Lockaby, is not talking. We have a man named Robert J. Snow in custody for false imprisonment of Mrs. Stella Williams.

"Now our witness stated that he feared that his life was in danger. The events of last night may prove him right. Three men broke into the Williamses' home. They were not there to burglarize the house. They were there to kidnap Timmy. The reason, I will get to later.

"They had in their possession a stun gun, a tranquilizer gun, handcuffs, and ropes. Items one would use in a kidnapping. Two of the three got away, but I believe they were killed in a car crash last night. The two men were driving a dark-colored van with Texas plates. The third man—I have his passport right here—Gunther Smit is his name. I am glad Joe Spinner is here because I think his forensics team will prove these things right. Gunther Smit is in custody, and he is not talking. These three men and Lockaby all worked for MPL, a company that has had several employees die or disappear. I am glad that Tom Willis is here because Timmy and Stella Williams have obtained the legal services of Jacob Weinstein."

The detective paused and took a sip of coffee. Lou looked around the room and tapped his pen.

"Tom, you have to go through Jacob Weinstein to talk to Timmy Williams. I need to speak with him too so maybe we can make an appointment with Weinstein. Okay?"

"I'll set something up with Jacob."

"Thanks, Tom. I think Timmy can tell us where . . . we can find Detective Simon's body. Just a feeling. Now comes the hard part. Why is this research company, MPL, hiring these criminals to hold people at gunpoint, to murder, to kidnap, and to break into houses? There is a rumor of a silver can that has magic powers. But too much exposure will kill you. I cannot prove there is a can like this. I have never seen it. But the fact is, people have died because of the mystery surrounding the silver can.

"What I am telling you now is speculation. At this MPL place, something was developed or discovered, maybe by accident, that made them feel good, but then it turned and made them feel bad. They killed either themselves or each other. One of them who recognized the danger took the can and ran off with it. Maybe he drove through town and threw it out the window. Now, this is fact—Fred McGraw found something while walking his dog. Fred asked Timmy to bury it and not to touch it. Timmy said he did what Fred told him to do. That night, Fred killed his dog and his wife and himself. Why would a man do that? John Withers did the autopsy on Fred. John Withers killed himself after acting strangely. That is a fact."

The detective paused again and took another drink of coffee.

"So we have Fred and his wife, John Withers, Detective Simon, James Teeter, the two men that died in the van crash, and the people at MPL that died. Their deaths are all related somehow to this silver can.

The silver can I cannot prove to exist. Now the reason I believe MPL wants to kidnap Timmy is that he lived, and he reaped the benefits of the alleged can. All the others have died. MPL wants to study Timmy.

"I believe that the silver can is a real thing, and I believe it is dangerous. If it falls into the wrong hands, the consequences could be catastrophic. MPL is in Texas, so we need to contact the FBI. Questions?"

"What do you mean catastrophic?"

"Well, Chief, we do not know the full power of this alleged silver can. But this MPL company is going to extremes because of this silver can. I think it is something big. We need to contact the FBI. Questions?"

The chief stood up and said, "All right, gentlemen, let's get back to work. Tom, my office. Good work, Lou."

The detective's office emptied, leaving just the three-person task force.

"Bobbi, close the door. Sit down, and Sergeant, you sit down too. Bobbi, Sergeant Kelley and I believe there is power in the silver can. We have only touched where the can has been, and we have benefited from its power. The bag once held the silver can. My hand was in the bag for less than a minute, and the next day, I had a slight headache. But my arthritis was gone. Kelley carried the bag."

"Yes, I was the only one who handled the bag," Kelley said. "I took it from the crime scene to the evidence room."

"Bobbi, Kelley tells me he is a crappy bowler, but he bowled three games over two hundred on Saturday. My love life is better than ever, and I do not need my glasses. I believe it is the silver can."

"This is the secret you two share?"

"Yes, Bobbi. Now the reason I did not bring this up at the meeting . . ."

"They would not believe you, and it would discredit the whole investigation."

"You got it, Bobbi. This kid wore Coke-bottle glasses. He does not need them anymore. He was clumsy in gym class, and the coach said Timmy did some amazing physical feats. His grades improved so much the teachers thought Timmy was cheating. Timmy says he never touched the can."

"What are we waiting for? Let's get the bag from the evidence room and see if it can make us smart enough to solve this case."

"Bobbi's right, boss. Let's do it."

Lou sat there and pondered the thought.

"Do not call me boss. The reason I have not done that is because I do not know how much is too much."

The phone rang, and Bobbi answered it.

"Hello, yes, sir. I will tell him. Thank you. Goodbye." Bobbi hung up the phone. "That was the DA's office. Jacob Weinstein is coming in for a meeting at one at Tom Wills's office. He wants you there."

"Okay, we will talk about this later. It is almost noon. I better get something to eat and get ready for this meeting."

Lou got up and grabbed his coat. He looked at his two-team task force and gave them the thumbs-up signal and left.

"I don't think I'm a crappy bowler."

*   *   *

Detective Cameron sat in Tom Wills's office with Tom and Tom's boss, Stan Mason. There was a secretary ready to take notes. Tom looked at Lou and pointed to a seat on the side of the room, where Lou quickly moved. They were all waiting for Jacob Weinstein and company to arrive. Lou looked Tom's office over. It was ten times bigger than Lou's and was spacious with a high ceiling. It also had big windows with a view of the downtown area.

Lou checked his watch—two minutes before one. Stan Mason was a tough character and was ex-military. He had retired from the marines and started a new career in the DA's office. Stan looked much younger than his sixty years. Lou wondered what he would think of the silver can story.

Lou glanced at the secretary and turned away. She was well-dressed, and she had a look about her of complete competence.

It was one o'clock, and Jacob Weinstein walked into the room. He was dressed in a suit with an expensive overcoat draped across his arm. He removed his stylish hat and handed his hat and coat to one of the two younger men who accompanied him. Everyone except the secretary stood, and introductions and handshakes were exchanged. Then everyone sat down except Stan, who took an at-ease military position by the window. Lou looked down at his scruffy brown shoes. All the men in the office were wearing thousand-dollar suits and five-hundred-dollar shoes. Lou felt out of place like a rat in a mink store.

Tom Wills was a hardworking man from the west side of town and was no match for Jacob Weinstein. Weinstein was about Stan's age. He was very clean looking and carried an air of confidence. Weinstein was well educated and had a reputation as being smart and honest. Lou thought Timmy could probably sense the qualities that Weinstein had and what he could do for his mother and himself.

Tom started talking, but soon Weinstein took over.

"We represent Tim and Stella Williams. They are in hiding because they fear for their lives. Mr. Wills, you and Mr. Mason put in writing what you want from my client, and he has agreed to cooperate fully. But my client has one request. Does anyone know what organization employed the man called Lockaby?"

Tom Wills looked at Lou.

"Yes, sir. Myers, Passmore, and Larkin, a chemical research company out of Austin, Texas."

"Thank you, Detective. My client requests a complete investigation of the company. He feels there is something criminal and, in my client's words, evil about this company and the way they do business. My client also feels there is a danger to our country. Again, in his words, catastrophic results could happen."

Tom looked at Lou and turned to Stan, and they whispered.

"Excuse me, sir, may I speak?"

All eyes turned to the detective with the stocky body and the wire-rimmed glasses.

"I believe in what Mr. Weinstein's client says. I listed the people who have died because of what Timmy Williams has said. I did not believe him, but now I do. Mr. Weinstein, sir, please tell your client I believe him."

"Detective, I will inform my client what you have said. I think we will leave you to your decision, Tom and Stan." Jacob stood up and walked over to Lou. "Remain seated, Detective." The rich man shook the hand of the cop. "Tom, you know how to reach me."

Jacob and company left the room.

Stan sat down and dismissed the secretary.

"Detective Cameron, may I call you Lou?"

"Yes, of course."

"Call me Stan. Tom, you want to hear this? Off the record."

"Yes, let me pull up a chair. I have heard some of the stories, so you believe in this silver can?"

"I do not want you to think I'm a nut."

"I'm not here to judge you," Stan said, "nor is Tom. We want the truth."

"I am afraid that if the silver can falls into the wrong hands, it can be an evil weapon."

"Do you know the location of the silver can?"

"No." Lou suddenly did not feel comfortable telling all he knew about the can. "I think I told Tom all I know in the briefing we had at ten this morning."

"You are not holding anything back? You aren't afraid to be labeled a nut for believing in the mystery of this silver can?"

Lou did not want to tell them about his arthritis or Kelley's bowling game; he just wanted to get out of that office.

"Timmy Williams is the one you need to talk with about the can. I do think you should contact the FBI and have them look into that MPL company."

"What should we tell them?" Stan said. "Some kid thinks they are a danger to the United States government?"

"You could tell them about the people that have died. You could tell them how Timmy has changed because of his exposure to the silver can. Imagine an army of men with the powers that Timmy possesses."

"And what are those powers, Detective?" asks Stan.

"He is more intelligent and more athletic to start with, and I think he knew the numbers for the lottery. Where else would he get the money to hire Jacob Weinstein?" Lou looked both men over. "Am I free to go?"

"Yes, of course, Lou. We will be in touch with you, and thanks for your input today." Tom shook Lou's hand and walked him to the door.

Lou was happy to get out of that office. He hustled down the hall and pushed the button for the elevator.

"I hear you believe."

Lou started to turn.

"Don't turn around," the voice said.

The elevator stopped, and they got in.

Lou turned and saw a young man with a hoodie and sunglasses. The young man took off the glasses and pulled back the hood.

"Timmy."

CHAPTER 4-4

THE RIDE

"I had no intentions of scaring you, but as long as you believe, I thought we should talk. I have a car waiting for us in the back. We will ride around and talk, and then you will be returned to wherever you want. Is that okay?"

"Yes."

The elevator stopped in the basement, and Lou followed Timmy to a waiting car. Once they were in the car, the driver sped away.

"Detective, our driver's name is Raymond. He is trustworthy and loyal. We must be careful. You know that."

"Yes, I know. How did you know I became a believer? Some magic from the silver can?"

"No, Jacob called me."

"Oh, can I ask you a few questions?" asked Lou.

"Yes, and then I have a few for you."

"That sounds fair. Do you know where Detective Simon's body is?"

"No."

"How can we find the body?" Lou asked.

"I do not know."

"How has your health been, and have you had any new powers that you can attribute to the silver can?"

"My health is good. I do not have any new powers. Now, can you tell me if Lockaby is his real name?" Tim asked.

"Yes, it is. He worked for MPL out of Texas."

"Where in Texas?"

"Near Austin."

"Is the DA's office going to contact the FBI?" asked Tim.

"Timmy, I do not think so. I have a feeling Stan Mason wants to recover the can and sell it to the military. I gave him an idea when I tried to scare him into calling the FBI."

"Who is Stan Mason?"

"Ex-military, DA. I told him that the silver can, in the wrong hands, could make a super army."

"And?"

"Stan started to drool. I am sure he has contacts in Washington."

"This is getting out of hand. I thought it was this MPL company we had to fight. Now it looks like we may have to fear our own government."

There was a long pause. Both Timmy and Lou were feeling hopeless.

"Just before Lockaby killed Jimmy Tee, he said I did not know my capabilities. Capabilities? What does Lockaby know?"

"Would you like to interview him?" the detective asked.

"No. Why do you believe me about the can? What changed your mind?"

"Arthritis. It had bothered my hands. The next day after I had my hand in that bag, I had a slight headache, and I could open and close my hands without pain. There were a few other things where my body's improved. I do not need these glasses anymore. Sergeant Kelley, the man who carried the bag from the woods to the evidence room, said his bowling game is much better."

"Oh, this is news to me. You do not have to have direct contact with the can. You are saying the residue from the can stayed in the bag and it cured your arthritis. That is interesting."

"Do you know where the can is now?" asked Lou.

"I'd rather not say."

"Drop me off at the police station."

"Raymond, take us to a block away from the police station. Detective, I'll call you. I have your number. Call Weinstein if you need to contact me."

*   *   *

Detective Cameron walked into his office. Bobbi and Kelley gave Lou a quick look then pretended they were working. Lou noticed Bobbi's clothes was a little disheveled.

"I don't want to know."

"We . . ." Bobbi started to say.

"I do not want to hear it." Then Lou saw Fred's bag. He also saw the Coors beer can. It was empty.

"I'm going home. Well, actually, I am going to see the peanut butter and jelly lady. Please return your toys to the evidence room," Lou said then left the room.

Lou pulled into Lilly's driveway and looked at his watch. Five thirty, early for Lou to be calling it a day. He knocked on the door, and a smiling Lilly opened the door.

"Hi, Lou, I did not expect you yet. Did you miss me?"

Lou walked in and put his arms around Lilly. He held her tight.

"Tough day? Come in and sit down. Want a beer?"

Lou went in and sat at the kitchen table. Lilly opened the fridge and put a Coors beer on the table. Lou saw a flashlight on the table.

"Here they are. I knew there were some batteries somewhere."

Lilly opened the flashlight and set the old batteries on the table. She put the new batteries into the flashlight and put the flashlight on the counter. Lou looked at the old batteries and picked one up in one hand then picked up the beer in the other hand. His eyes went back and forth.

"Could be. This could be."

"What did you say, Lou?"

"A round cylinder with no opening. Like a battery."

"I ordered a pizza. It should be here at six."

Lou wondered what Tim would think of his idea.

"Earth to Lou, come in please."

"Sorry, Lilly. I had a rough day. Pizza at six. What's for dessert?"

"TA-DA," Lilly said with her arms wide open.

Lou started to laugh. He used to be a serious man, but Lilly made him laugh. Laughing felt good, and now he had an idea about the silver can. This idea made him happy too because Lou felt like he was on to something.

The next morning, the detective sat in his office. Bobbi and Kelley had not arrived, so Lou went to the evidence room and brought the bag and now-empty beer can back to his desk. He was sitting with the bag when Bobbi came in the office.

"Lou, I'm—"

"Stop, I don't want to hear it. I am more interested in finding out if touching the bag and drinking the beer helped improve your police skills."

Kelley walked in and looked at Lou and shook his head in disgrace.

"Okay you two. You can call me boss because I am the boss of this investigation. I hope that whatever happened yesterday stays in yesterday."

"I have a headache," Bobbi said.

"Me too," replied Kelley.

"I hope the bag and the beer were good. We are going to do some old-fashioned police work. Bobbi, I want you to check all the phone records of Lockaby and Detective Simon since the time the two met. Kelley, take a uniformed officer and go where Lockaby was staying and ask questions. Then go to where Simon lived and knock on doors. Use the power of the silver can. Trust your gut get some answers. I should have done this before, but then again, we do not know if Detective Simon is dead. And I want to know if the bag or the beer is working for you or if I am wasting my time on this bag."

"Okay, boss. I'm on it," Sergeant Kelley said as he left the office.

"Me too, boss," Bobbi said before she left the office.

Lou reached into his coat pocket and pulled out an unopened can of Coors beer. Lou put the beer into the bag and removed the empty can and squashed it with his bare hands and put it in his coat pocket. The detective then took the bag with the full can of beer back to the evidence room. Lou returned just in time to catch the ringing phone in his office.

"Hello, Detective Cameron here." Lou made his way around his desk and sat down. "Okay, Tom. That upsets me. Is this Stan's idea? Well, you go to the FBI then. Go over Stan's head. Tom, Tom, I will tell you why I believe. I had arthritis in my hands. I had a hard time with buttons. I had my hand in the bag that this alleged silver can was buried in for less than a minute, and now my arthritis is gone."

Lou held the phone away from his ear. Tom was making the argument of how that did not prove it had anything to do with the can.

"Okay, Tom, if you are not going to move on this, then goodbye." Lou hung up the phone. Bobbi walked in the office.

"I might have something. The last call to Detective Simon that Lockaby made was just before Simon went missing. After that, there were no more calls to Simon. Lockaby knew Simon was dead, so why call him? Lockaby made one call to a Jack Passmore in Austin, Texas, after his last call to Simon. That call was twenty minutes long. Jack Passmore is the CEO of MPL."

"Thanks, Bobbi. The DA's office won't go to the FBI about the MPL company."

"Why not?"

"Not enough evidence. Tom Wills called and gave me the news. Stan says no, and that is the one request Timmy made to Jacob Weinstein for complete cooperation in this investigation. What other calls did Lockaby have on his phone after he last talked to Simon?"

"There is one on here to the dead body removal company. Only joking, boss, sorry."

"Bobbi, what if Lockaby called this Jack Passmore guy and he called the dead body removal company?"

"I'll get Passmore's phone records. I may need a lawyer's permission slip."

"A subpoena. Go to the chief and tell him I think Stan is trying to block this investigation and get that subpoena from a friendly judge."

"Okay, boss."

"I need the number for Jacob Weinstein. Do you have it?"

"In your desk is a phone book. You can spell, can't ya, Lou?" Then Bobbi disappeared out the door.

Lou reached in the drawer, and there was the phone book. He pulled it out and started looking. "I thought I was the boss."

The chief entered Lou's office and closed the door. He sat in the chair in front of Lou. Police Chief William Gibson was a quiet man in his sixties. He took a long look at Lou, and Lou looked right back at him.

"Tell me, Lou, why do you think Stan is trying to block the investigation?"

"Stan wants to find that silver can and sell to the Pentagon. I am sure he has friends there. Profit. If he can locate the can, then he could sell it and make money. That is why Stan is holding up the investigation."

"Where is your proof?"

The chief was a man of few words and went right to the point.

"With that can, Stan thinks he can have an army of supersoldiers. This silver can made a clumsy, average fourteen-year-old into an A student and an athlete. Maybe I am exaggerating but not by much. It cured my arthritis. It made my love life a hell of a lot better. And all I did was put my hand in the bag that held the can."

"My wife would like that. Not the arthritis part but the other part."

"Chief, I challenge you right now. Go down to the evidence room. It is in aisle twenty-one. Put your hands in the bag for a minute, and if there is any magic left, you will know it."

The chief got up and left. Bobbi came in.

"I was outside the door and heard everything. Lou, you're gonna have a stampede down in the evidence room if word gets out. You should have used the sex angle from the beginning, and this case would be solved by now."

"I hope there is still some magic in the old bag."

"There was last night."

"Enough, Bobbi. I do not want to hear it."

"Okay, boss, did you get to call Weinstein?"

"No."

Bobbi turned to her computer, punched it a few times, wrote down the number, and took it to Lou.

"Want me to dial it for you, boss?"

"Just give me the number!"

"Oh, touchy. Want to make a bet? I say the chief goes home early today."

Lou dialed the Weinstein number.

"Hello, this is Detective Cameron. Could I speak with Jacob Weinstein? Yes, I would like to leave a message. I need to talk with Timmy. It is essential. Have him call me. Immediately. Goodbye."

Kelley walked into the office. Lou stood up.

"Let's go eat. I'm buying, and I'm driving."

"Where are we going, boss?"

"One-Eyed Jack's, a table in the back and some privacy. No business till we are done eating."

Lou's phone rang. Bobbi picked it up.

"Detective Lou Cameron's office. Hold please."

"If it's not Timmy, take a message and I will call them back."

"Yes, Sheriff, can I take a message? He will call you back. Okay, what is your number?" Bobbi took the message and put it on Lou's desk.

Bobbi hung up the phone, and it rang again. It was Timmy, and Bobbi handed the phone to Lou.

"Hello, can you meet me at One-Eyed Jack's? I'll be there in fifteen minutes."

The small group got into Lou's car and took the short ride to One-Eyed Jack's. Lou parked, and they walked into the restaurant. They were seated in the back and started looking over the menu.

"They are here," Lou said.

Bobbi and Kelley looked up and saw two men walking toward them. One man was in his early forties, dressed in dress pants, a blue shirt, and a light-brown jacket.

The other man was slimmer and shorter and wore blue jeans and a white hoodie. They sat down, and the smaller man pulled back his hoodie, revealing a young teenager.

"Bobbi, Kelley, this is Timmy. Yes, the famous Timmy. The gentleman with Timmy, if I remember, is Raymond. Timmy, this is my task force, Officer Bobbi Jackson and Sergeant Brian Kelley. Raymond, I know nothing about you. Here comes the waitress. Let's get our order in, and then we will talk."

"Anything we want?"

"Anything you want, Bobbi. You order it."

"Rack of ribs," Bobbi said.

"Me too," said Kelley.

"Me too," said Lou.

"I want a cheeseburger and French fries and a Pepsi."

"Typical teenager. What do you want, Raymond?"

"Go with the ribs. Lou's buying," Bobbi announced. "They are delicious. You won't regret it."

"Okay, ribs."

The waitress took the orders and went to the kitchen.

"Timmy, if you please, how did you meet Raymond?"

"Raymond is my . . ." Timmy choked up a little and could not speak.

Raymond put his arm around Timmy.

"Tim is my son. Are you okay, Tim?"

"Yes, Dad."

The members of the task force were stunned and touched. Bobbi had tears in her eyes.

"I did not know you were still in the picture," Lou said.

"Let me clear up a few things."

"You don't need to do that, Raymond."

"Yes, I do, Detective. Tim has gone through a lot of changes because of the silver can, but he is still a fourteen-year-old boy. I have remained in touch with him and his mother. Yes, I abandoned my family and ran off. I started a new life and that went belly-up, and I was too ashamed to come back. I had a dead-end job making minimum wage. Stella wrote and asked for help. I came as fast as I could. I know I must earn everyone's trust. But please do not doubt my love for my son."

"Raymond, let me say that we at this table do not doubt your love for your son."

"Hear, hear," said Bobbi and was echoed by Kelley as they banged their hands on the table.

"Here comes the food. Timmy, you are going to wish you ordered ribs," said Bobbi.

The food was on the table, and everyone was eating and making small talk. When the meal was over, Raymond asked a question.

"May I make a statement?"

Everyone shut up and gave him the floor.

Raymond stood up and held out his glass of water and said, "I propose a toast to my son, Tim, who wants to be known as Tim, not that childish name Timmy. And I want to be addressed as Ray, not that adult name of Raymond."

The group first said cheers, then it was a chant of "Hear, Hear" and the banging of silverware on plates.

"Okay, Sergeant Kelley, report," Lou said.

"The day after Detective Simon disappeared, a blue Chevy van with Texas plates was seen in the area. It was a Chevy van like the one that those two men died in at that accident. Witnesses remember Lockaby in the same area. And the reason they remember Lockaby is because he dressed in those shiny black suits and stood straight as an arrow. Now the area where they saw him was on Gale Street, a block away from where Robert J. Snow lives and two blocks away from where James Teeter, alias Jimmy Tee, lived before he died."

"What is your gut feeling on this, Sergeant?"

"I think Lockaby killed Detective Simon because he may have found out Lockaby was not a government agent. I think Teeter and Snow helped hide the body until this van from Texas came and took the body away."

"How good are your witnesses?"

"Mabel Jenkins owns the corner diner, and she was there when Lockaby came in and sat down with Teeter and Snow. She will testify to it. Across the street is a gas station run by Ron Jones, and he remembers the Texas plates because he was born in Texas. That is why it stuck out to him, and he is willing to testify."

"Bobbi checked phone records of Lockaby's cell. And tomorrow, we may have a subpoena, a permission slip, to check some phone records in Texas."

"Boss, you are doing fine."

"Thanks, Bobbi. If they took Detective Simon's body to Texas, we might never see it again. They might have chemicals that render a human body unidentifiable."

"These are bad people?" asked Ray.

"That they are, Ray. Now, Tim, you have seen the silver can. You may be the only one alive besides Lockaby that has seen the silver can and is still alive. Let us all think outside the box. What if the MPL company did not make the silver can? What if that silver can was made somewhere else? Say another world. What if it came from outer space and someone found it and took it to MPL because they are a research company? And they went through the phases of happiness then headache and then craziness that ended in murder. And someone at MPL recognized the danger and took the can with the intent of destroying it, and they dumped it on the side of the road where Fred McGraw found it and brought it home."

"So what is the can?" asked Kelley.

"I think it is a battery. And it is radiating something, and if we get too much of it, we die. Tim had the right amount of what we want. Enough to make us healthier, smarter, more athletic, and have an ability to pick lotto numbers. If it is a battery, it has a life of so much time, but that could be one hundred years for all we know. What do you think, Tim?"

"I have been wasting my time. I have been thinking about how to destroy it. I should be thinking about how to use it. Find out how to shield it and make it safe."

"Is Tim still in danger?" asked Ray.

"Yes. Think you can get home safely?"

"Yes, Tim can sense danger."

"Wait, how did the can get here? Aliens?" asked Bobbi.

"Maybe it is one possibility," answered Lou.

"It could have fallen out of a jet pack or some machine they had. The aliens may not have noticed they lost it."

"That's a good possibility, Tim," added Lou.

Ray spoke up, "And we don't know what the long-term effects of this will be on Tim."

That had everyone's attention because they all had some exposure to the silver can. The thought of cancer or some other disease caused by the silver can now entered their minds.

"Okay, let's get out of here. Sergeant Kelley, fill out the report. I'll pay the bill, and I'll get the tip. Go home, everyone."

"We rode with you, boss," Bobbi reminded Lou.

"Oh, that's right, sorry."

Lou went back to his office and got ready to go home. He saw the note that Bobbi took. Sheriff Justin Smith, Tate County, Arizona. Lou wondered what that was about. He dialed the number.

CHAPTER 4-5

A FIGHT IN THE WOODS

Lou pulled into Lilly's driveway. There was a car sitting in the Williamses' driveway. Lou looked it over. Maybe a potential buyer. Lou walked up to Lilly's door, and it opened. Lilly stood there in an elegant black gown with a red rose clutched in between her teeth, and she began to dance. Lou heard music—"Baby, I Need Your Loving." Lilly took the rose out of her mouth.

"Johnny Rivers, I love this song." Lilly put the rose back in between her teeth and danced.

Lou came in and closed the door. He started shaking his behind and getting in the mood. The song ended with Lilly in Lou's arms.

"I love you, Lilly."

"About time you told me."

"Let's get married."

"Gee, Lou, you're getting the milk for free, and you want to marry the cow?"

"Yes, I do." Lou got down on one knee. "Will you marry me, Lilly?"

"Let me see, you come here to sleep in my bed, eat my peanut butter and jelly, and now you want to marry me. Of all the nerve, YES. Yes. I love you too, Lou. Let's play Johnny again. Thank you, Johnny Rivers, wherever you are."

Lilly ran and started the song again. She went back to Lou and started singing, "Baby, I need your loving. Baby, I need your loving. Got to have all your loving . . ."

Later, Lou and Lilly were lying in bed. Lou remembered the car next door.

"Lilly, whose car is that parked in the Williamses' driveway?"

"I don't know, but he had that military walk about him. He had a shovel and one of those metal detectors, I think."

Lou jumped out of bed and dressed as fast as he could. He dialed Bobbi and handed the phone to Lilly.

"Tell Bobbi to get Kelley and come over here as fast as possible."

Lou looked outside, and the car was still there. It was dark, but a full moon lit up the night. Lou remembered Lilly's flashlight and grabbed it and went outside toward the woods. Lou wandered around until he heard the shovel sliding into the dirt.

"Did you find it, Stan?"

Then Lou flashed the light on Stan.

"Look, Detective, don't you see what a weapon like this can be for our country? We can conquer the world."

"I thought we already did."

"Come on, Lou, we can sell it to the Pentagon and be rich."

"I think you better go home, Stan."

"You cannot imagine how many coins, pop tops, and pieces of junk I found trying to locate the can."

"Go home, Stan."

"Where is it, Lou? We could be rich. We can be partners."

"I don't know where it is, and I don't want to be partners. Go home."

"I'm coming over there and beating it out of you."

"I do not know where it is, and you would be wasting your time. Go home, Stan."

"I don't believe you. You must know the location of the can. You and your friend, that kid Timmy."

"Tim, he wants to be called Tim."

"What? I don't care. I'm going to kick your ass."

"Calm down, Stan, and go home."

"I've been digging out here in the dark. I'm a little frustrated. I want that CAN."

Stan dropped what he had in his hands and started walking toward Lou.

"I'm a marine, and you are a fat, out-of-shape cop. This should be easy."

Lou backed up a little and wondered what was taking Bobbi and Kelley so long to get here. Lou decided to hold his ground. *Use the power of the can,* he thought. Besides, he did not like Stan, and Stan needed a lesson. The anger started to build in Lou.

"You may be a marine, but I am one pissed-off cop. Come and get me."

Stan circled Lou and tried to land a few punches, but Lou was quick and fended them off. Stan was getting aggravated because he could not land a punch. Stan charged Lou, and Lou got in a combination of blows. And Stan went down. Stan got up slow. He was mad now. Stan started dancing around and swung his leg up to kick Lou in the head, but Lou ducked and grabbed Stan's leg. Lou held Stan's leg frozen in time.

"Go home, Stan," Lou said then pushed Stan to the ground using Stan's leg as the driving ram.

Stan got up and ran over to where he had some equipment. He pulled out a gun and took a shot at Lou. Lou jumped, and the bullet missed. Lou heard a moan. He ran back toward the cry.

"LILLY, NO, NO."

Lilly s shot. Lou reaches for his gun, but all he found was that crushed up beer can. Lou pulled it out. Stan stood there in shock that he had shot someone. Lou led with his left foot and threw the beer can, which hit Stan in the torso. Stan went down. Lou turned and went to Lilly's side and picked her up and headed for the car. Bobbi and Kelley finally had arrived.

"What's going on, boss?" asked an alarmed Bobbi.

"Stan shot Lilly. Get us to the hospital. Sergeant Kelley, Stan is out there in the woods. He has a weapon. Better get backup. Bobbi, drive."

"Kelley, call ahead for me, please!" Bobbi yelled.

Kelley got on his cell. "I want to report a shooting on Dublin Road. The victim is en route to the hospital with Detective Cameron. No, it's a woman. Her first name is Lilly. That's all I know. I'm at the McGraw house on Dublin Road. The suspect is Stan Mason. He is in the woods. Okay, goodbye."

Then Kelley went back in the woods. He found Stan with a wadded-up beer can in his chest. Kelley kicked Stan's gun away. Stan moved his arm slightly. Kelley then got back on his cell.

"I need an ambulance on Dublin Road and a forensic squad. Suspect in custody."

Kelley saw the lights and heard the sirens. Backup had arrived. Kelley made one more call then turned the investigation over to one of his colleagues. Sergeant Kelley headed for the hospital.

Sergeant Kelley arrived at the hospital and hustled his way to where the group was waiting. Lilly was having surgery. He came down the hall and saw Bobbi, who came to meet him.

Lou sat in a chair all by himself, wringing his hands over and over. Tom Wills was sitting with Police Chief Gibson.

"How is she doing?"

"She is having a tough time, Kelley," answered Bobbi.

"How is Lou doing?'

"Lou is—"

Bobbi was interrupted when the medics came rushing down the hall with a man on a gurney. It was Stan Mason. Uniformed officers were accompanying the gurney. Tom Wills and Chief Gibson went over to Sergeant Kelley.

"Sergeant, can you fill us in on what happened?" asked the chief. "After they left for the hospital."

"I called for backup then went out in the woods and found Stan Mason with a gun by his side. He was on his back and had a round object imbedded in his chest."

"What was Stan doing in the woods?" asked the chief.

"Looking for the DAMN CAN," Bobbi said in an upset, pissed-off voice. Then she ran into the ladies' room.

"Chief, Stan was obsessed about that can. He wanted it bad," said Tom.

Bobbi came out of the ladies' room and squatted in front of Lou, but before she could say a word, she saw the pool of blood dripping from Lou's hands.

"HEY, somebody, Doctor, Nurse. This man is bleeding!" yelled Bobbi.

A nurse came over and promptly took Lou into a room.

"I thought it was Lilly's blood, but Lou's hands were bleeding."

The chief, Tom, and Kelley went over to Bobbi.

A doctor came out with a small pan, and in that pan was a wadded-up piece of metal. The metal was in the shape of a ball.

"This is what we pulled out of Mr. Mason's chest," the doctor said. "He will live, but he has a hole in his chest an inch deep."

"What is it?" asked Tom.

"My guess is . . . an empty can of beer squashed in to a ball. Coors, I would guess. You want it?"

"Yes, one of you officers take this and put it in an evidence bag." The chief commanded. "Thanks, Doctor. Your patient is the shooter, so we will put him under arrest and have two men guarding him."

The doctor nodded and walked away.

"That is why Lou's hands were bleeding," Kelley said. "He didn't have a gun, so he squeezed a beer can down to a ball and threw it, kind of remarkable. Chief, I believe Bobby Snow knows Lockaby killed Detective Simon and helped Lockaby hide the body. We have that van with Texas plates. It's a little wrecked, but that should have all kinds of evidence that will help solve the case."

"I believe you. Your dad would be proud."

"Thanks, Chief. I will file my report and work with forensics. The DA's office should have plenty of evidence to work with."

"Tom, talk with Sergeant Kelley. He's got the Simon case well in hand. And Tom, I want you to go to the FBI and think of something, use the disappearance of Detective Simon to get them to investigate the MPL company."

"Okay, Chief."

Lou came out of the room with his hands bandaged.

"Any news on Lilly?" asked Lou.

Bobbi came over to Lou and took him by the arm. "Not yet."

"I'll tell you, Bobbi, what happened, and you can tell the chief or Tom. Stan went there for the can. He wanted to sell it to the Pentagon. I told him no. We got into a fight. Stan pulled a gun and shot Lilly, and I threw a beer can that knocked him down. I got Lilly and ran to the road, and you know the rest."

"Okay, Lou, I'll file the report."

Out came a doctor.

"Who's here for Lilly Turner?"

"Right here, Doctor," answered Lou.

"Let's go somewhere private."

"Doctor, say what you have to say. I have to know."

"Well, all right," the doctor said as he first looked at the floor then looked straight into Lou's eyes. "The bullet was close to her heart, and it was touch and go. But she came through the operation amazingly well. Still, I think it is fifty-fifty. She is asleep now. What is your relationship with Mrs. Turner?"

"She is my fiancée."

"Oh, Lou," cried Bobbi.

"You can wait in her room. I'll get a nurse to take you," said the doctor.

A nurse came over and took Lou away to be with Lilly. Bobbi ran over to where Kelley, Tom, and the chief were standing.

"Lou and Lilly were going to get married. I do not know if I should be happy or sad."

"That was sudden. Didn't Lou meet Lilly recently?" asked the chief.

"Yes, but it feels right doesn't it, Bobbi?"

"It sure does, Sergeant Kelley."

"I'm going home, but I will be back first thing in the morning. Call me if there is any change." The chief said good night and left.

Tom said, "Me too. Good night."

"I'm staying."

"Me too, Bobbi," said Kelley.

Lou was dozing in Lilly's room, exhausted from the day's events, when he heard voices. He awoke and saw two doctors standing over Lilly.

"Yeah, hold it there for five seconds, and if we need to do it longer, we will," Lou heard one of the doctors say.

"What is going on?" Lou said, waking up.

"Lou, it's us."

Lou looked up and saw Tim and Ray dressed in green.

Tim spoke, "Lou, we are trying a little silver can medicine. We put a cloth next to the can for an hour, and now we have placed it on Lilly for five seconds. I'm giving it to you in a plastic sandwich bag. If she needs more, do it again."

"Is that safe?" asks Lou.

"I think so. What do you think, Dr. Dad?"

"I agree with Dr. Tim. Five seconds at a time but only as needed. Hold it over the wound. Then put it back in the plastic bag. Fred McGraw had a cloth bag, but we have found that it does not radiate through plastic."

"Are you sure? Do you know what you're doing? I love that woman."

"I know it is safe. I am as sure as I was the day I picked the lotto numbers."

"We would never take a chance on someone's life," said Ray. "Have some faith in the silver can. Bobbi says you are getting married. Tim has a wedding gift for you and Lilly."

Tim put a check in Lou's shirt pocket.

"Where is the can? Sorry, never mind."

"It is in a safe location. Dad and I dug it up and moved it a few days ago. It is wrapped in plastic and in a safe location. Dad, Mom, and I are going to disappear, and the only way to reach us is though Jacob Weinstein. You are a good man, Detective."

"That goes double from me," Ray said. "Goodbye, Lou, and good luck."

Then Tim and his father disappeared. Lou was still not fully awake. Did that happen, or was that a dream? Lou looked at the plastic sandwich bag in his hand that contained the small slip of cloth. Lou stood up and looked at Lilly. She was breathing easier than she did last night.

Lou went out to the hallway. He saw the room where two uniformed police men were standing. Lou went over and showed his badge and went in to see Stan. Stan was asleep. Lou took out the cloth and held it over Stan's wound for five seconds and then put it back in the plastic bag and stuck it back into his pocket Stan woke up, and he looked at Lou.

"I'm sorry, Lou. How is the lady?"

"I have faith she is going to be all right."

"Thank God. I lost my head. I was foolish. Please forgive me, Lou."

"I already did. Now listen to me. It was an accidental shooting. You and I had a disagreement that escalated to a fight, and the gun went off. Agree?"

"Yes, sure. Why are you doing this, Lou?"

"I do not know. But you must forget about the silver can and stop thinking of it as a weapon. How does your chest feel?"

"Good, no pain. What did you do? I feel great."

"Goodbye, Stan. I'll talk to the chief."

Lou left the room and saw Bobbi and Kelly asleep in chairs. He did not disturb them. Lou got a cup of coffee and went back to Lilly's room.

"Hi, Lou."

"Lilly, you're awake. How do you feel?"

"Not too bad after being shot last night."

"You still want to marry a cop?"

"Only if we can have peanut butter and jelly sandwiches at the reception and we have to have a band that can play 'Baby I Need Your Loving.'"

"We can do that."

The doctor came in. "Well, I did not expect you to be awake yet. How do you feel, Mrs. Turner?"

"Excellent, and soon you will be calling me Mrs. Cameron."

"Wow, congratulations. Let me look at the wound here. Amazing. No redness and starting to heal already. It is my professional opinion, Lilly, that you are going to make a full recovery. Funny, the man that they brought in last night is doing amazingly well also. Better than he should be. Something funny is going on. I do not care if my patients get well. I must go and make my rounds."

The doctor left, and Bobbi and Kelley came into the room and caught Lou and Lilly kissing.

"Hey, you two, get a room!" yelled Bobbi.

"We have one," said Lilly.

They all laughed. Bobbi grabbed Lilly by the hand, and then they embraced.

Kelley stood back but could not hide the pleasure on his face. Lou looked at Kelley.

"It was you that called Tim, wasn't it?" Lou asked.

"I called Jacob Weinstein."

"In the middle of the night? And you got through?" asked Lou.

"Police emergency worked."

"Thanks, Sergeant."

The chief walked in.

"I heard the laughter down the hall. I guess everyone is doing well."

"Yes, Chief. Let's call this an accidental shooting."

"You sure you want it that way, Lou? What do you say, Lilly?"

"The man was not aiming at me. It could have been a warning shot, and I was in the way. I did have that black gown on. Besides, I have a wedding to plan, and I do not want to be tied up in court. Bobbi, would you want to help with the wedding?"

"Oh, yes, yes."

The two ladies giggled like girls. The chief motioned to Lou. The chief and Lou went to the side of the room and whispered, "I believe in the silver can. You can have that subpoena if you still need it."

"I knew you would become a believer, Chief. I'm taking some time off. Lilly's going to need me, and we're getting married. Sergeant Kelley is capable and deserves a promotion. So does Bobbi. Give Stan a chance. I would not be too hard on him. Okay?"

"Okay, Lou."

Lou went over to where Bobbi and Kelley were.

"You two must have a lot of paperwork to do."

"Okay, Lou. We can take a hint," Bobbi said.

"Whatever happened to calling me boss. I thought it made you feel important."

"Okay, boss. We are out of here. Come on, Sergeant Kelley."

"Later, boss."

"Later, Kelley."

"Alone at last, but no peanut butter and jelly."

"Oh, I forgot. Tim and his father left us a wedding gift,"

"Lou. Who are Tim and his father? And who was that man last night? And what is this silver can he was digging for?"

"Guess I have some explaining to do."

Lou took the check that Tim gave him out of his shirt pocket. He looked at it and handed it to Lilly. She opened it up and stared at the amount.

"Oh my."

"Okay, Lilly, we never talked about this, and we should. Why do you think your dad did what he did?"

"Lou, my mom smoked constantly. I think she was dying. My dad did not want her to suffer, and he wanted to go with her. And that gives me comfort."

"Lilly, did the Williams family live there when you were still living at home?"

"No, but I knew Stella a little from visiting my parents."

"Tim is Stella's son, and Ray is the father. Your father found what looked like a beer can. It was not a beer can. We called it the silver can because that is what it looked like. This silver can causes changes in the human body. All that touched it died. Your father must have recognized the danger. He asked Tim to bury it and not tell anyone about it."

"Is this silver can what killed my parents?" asked Lilly.

"Yes, Lilly, I think it is. I can't prove it. I have not seen the alleged can. I know it sounds crazy, but it gets even crazier. Things that touch the can seem to absorb some of its power and transfer it to someone else, like the sheets we've been sleeping on."

"Oh, Lou, I knew there was something going on when I first lay on them."

"I received a phone call today from a sheriff in Arizona. He thinks Fred's death is related to some deaths out in Arizona."

"What do you think, Lou? I'd like to know the reason why my father would shoot my mother."

"Well, this Arizona sheriff says he had been chasing down every lead on deaths that fit a certain circumstance. He knows about MPL Chemical Company in Austin, Texas."

"Lou, what does the MPL Chemical Company have to do with this?"

Lou laughed. "This is going to be a long night. Lilly, I'll tell you a story. It seems that I don't know the beginning or the end. I must call this sheriff and maybe even fly down there. I must find out if what he is telling me is the truth."

"Do it, Lou. Find out the truth. Go to Arizona. I'll heal and get well, and then we are going to get married."

"Sounds like a plan, Lilly."

PART FIVE

EVERYONE WANTS
THE SILVER CAN

CHAPTER 5-1

PEOPLE ARE CRAZY

The small group had gathered in the home of Lilly and Lou to celebrate their wedding. Everyone wore the appropriate clothing, but it was not a fancy affair. The group was seated at folding tables in the living room. The meal was complete, and Sergeant Brian Kelley picked up a spoon and clanged it against a wine glass. He then stood up and cleared his throat.

"As best man, I guess this is where I make a speech. I want to go around the table and introduce everyone. Judge Brown and his wife, Nancy, sweet service, Judge. Chief of police William Gibson and his wife, Barbra, and Roberta 'Bobbi' Jackson."

"You better call me Bobbi," Bobbi said with a laugh.

There were some chuckles around the table, and then Kelley continued.

"We have with us Ray, Stella, and Tim Williams. Good to have you here. I know Lou and Lilly are glad you could make it. Our caterers, Fay and Tina, come out here. They are hiding in the kitchen."

The two ladies came to the doorway. Lou and Lilly stood and led the applause.

"Excellent meal," Lou added. "They even made our favorite little peanut butter and jelly sandwiches. Sorry, Brian, I'll sit back down."

"Thanks, Lou." Kelley paused a moment. "Now, I have to say something nice about Lou and Lilly, the new Mr. and Mrs. Louis Cameron."

"Here, here," Bobbi cheered and banged on the table.

Everyone clapped and cheered. The attention then went back on Kelley.

"Lou and Lilly are two beautiful people. They found each other, and they have changed each other. They also have changed those around them. All for the better, by the way. Truth, honesty, loyalty—that is Lou. He is modest and fair, and I would trust Lou with my life. Lilly, you have breathed life into Lou, into us, and into what we call life. We love your sense of humor and what you have done to Lou. I want to make a toast to Lou and Lilly."

Everyone stood and raised a glass.

"To a happy and long life. May all your dreams come true. To Lou and Lilly."

"To Lou and Lilly," repeated everyone, and Bobbi and Tim led the pounding on the table. Bobbi smiled at Tim. It was one of the first times Bobbi saw the young man enjoy himself.

Lilly remained standing when everyone sat down.

"I'd like to say something. I want to thank everyone for everything. I had a big wedding the first time. So this time is sweet and speacial. A lot has happened since I met Lou. I fell in love. I got shot. I spent some time in the hospital. And in two more weeks, Lou and I are going to travel. The loved ones that are not here, Lou and I are going to visit. I have a brother in Ohio, a daughter in Flordia, and a son in Alaska. Lou has a daughter in New Zealand. I look forward to introducing Lou to my family and getting to meet his family. Is there anything you want to say, Lou?"

"No."

There was laughter around the table.

"Smart move, Lou," said Bobbi.

"I want to thank Bobbi for helping me prepare and plan for this day. There is a little room for dancing, and Tim has agreed to be our DJ."

Tim got up and turned on the music. The first song was "Baby I Need Your Loving." Lou and Lilly got up and danced. Ray and Stella soon joined them. Fay and Tina were clearing the tables to make more room. Everyone joined in, and the folding tables were taken down.

The secound song was "Mustang Sally," and everyone was dancing. Judge Brown and his wife were getting into the party. Tim took turns dancing with Fay and Tina.

"Who picked this song?" Lou asked. "Bobbi?"

"Lou, I did," answered Lilly.

The party started to wind down, and Tim and Lou found themselves alone in the kitchen.

"Tim, I went to Arizona and talked with Sheriff Smith, whom I have been telling you about. I met and talked with someone or something who called himself Dr. Dunn. That is not his real name. He claims he is an alien. Lilly knows I went to Arizona, but only you and I know about Dr. Dunn. Dr. Dunn wants the can back. He says it belongs on his planet and it was his mistake to have lost it here. The earth will be a lot safer with what he calls a spoola back in his world."

"Dad and I think we can help people with the can. We are learning how to control it. I may be a dreamer, but I want to use the silver can to do good."

"You are a dreamer. I think you want to do the right thing. But the dangers far outweigh the good."

"Can I call you Lou?"

"That's what my name is. And yes, you may."

"Lou I'd like to study the silver can. I think if we can control its power, we can achieve great things."

"I was asked if it was in a safe place. I was asked to talk you into giving it back to Dr. Dunn. He wants to take it back to his planet and keep it safe because if it falls into the wrong hands, there is no telling what destruction it could do. This could effect the whole world."

"I know, but I do not want to let it go. I will think about what you said."

"Please do, Tim. If the government gets control of it, they will make it a weapon of war. And Dr. Dunn says he will never get it back if that happens. Dr. Dunn gave me this tracking device." Lou pulled it out of his pocket. "It looks like a stone. If I need him, I'm supposed to squeeze it and he will come."

"Lilly said you were going on your honeymoon in two weeks. I'll have to decide before then. Lou, are you sure this is not a scheme to get the can for Russia or China or some evil in the world?"

"Sheriff Smith said how reluctant he was to tell anyone about his encounter with a spaceman. I know that feeling. Tim, I think Dr. Dunn knows a lot about the silver can. I believe he brought it here, and he can take it away."

"Okay, Lou, we will make arrangements later this week."

"Come on, Tim, let's get back to the party. You are the DJ. Play a sweet song."

*　　*　　*

Lou and Lilly sit in the kitchen by themselves. The last guest had gone home.

"That was a wonderful party," said Lilly.

"Let's go to bed, Mrs. Cameron."

"Yes, Mr. Cameron."

CHAPTER 5-2

THE NEWS

The next morning, Lou got out of bed. He looked out of the window and saw a dark van parked across the street.

"Lilly, I'm going down to the store and pick up a paper. Is there anything you want?"

"No," answered Lilly. "You won't be long, will you?"

"Ten minutes."

"I'll get up and start breakfast."

"I'll cook something when I get back."

Lilly jumped out of bed.

"I don't think so. I have had your cooking before. You go and get back, and I'll cook."

"Okay." Lou got dressed and walked out to his car. He did not like the dark van across the street. Lou pulled out of the driveway, and the van followed. Lou pulled into the store parking lot. The black van went down the street. Lou went into the store and picked up the paper.

Don, the store owner, said to Lou, "Your picture is in the paper, Lou."

"Oh," Lou said as he put his money on the counter. Lou looked at the paper. He looked at Don and then looked back at the paper. Lou walked out of the store, and they were waiting.

"Detective Cameron, what can you tell us about the silver can?" asked a woman with a microphone in her hand. Behind her was a camera crew filming everything. Lou did not say anything. He pushed his way through the people and got in his car.

"Where did all these people come from?" Lou asked himself. "They were not here when I pulled in." Lou backed his car out and went home, only to find more film crews waiting for him. Lou pulled into his driveway and pushed his way though the people.

"Detective Cameron, how magical is the silver can?" yelled a man.

Lou made it inside and locked the door. He then realized he left the newspaper in the car. The phone was ringing.

"Don't answer it," said Lilly. "Lou, can we unplug the phone? You still have your cell."

Lou picked up the phone.

"Hello," Lou listened about ten seconds and hung it up. He then unplugged the phone from the wall. Lou sat down at the kitchen table.

"Coffee is hot, and how do you want your eggs? Who was on the phone?"

"CNN. Scammbled eggs sound good today. They want to interview me."

"Who, the eggs?" Lilly said with a smile.

Lou laughed. His head then slumped forward.

"My cell is buzzing."

"Eat your eggs, and then you can do what you want with the phone."

Lilly placed a plate of scrammbled eggs on the table. Lou picked up his fork and dug into the eggs. Lilly set a cup of black coffee on the table, and then she sat down. They began eating.

"Lilly, we should pack a few things and leave town."

There was a knock on the door. Lou and Lilly ignored it.

"Lou, honey, I think you are right."

The pounding on the door became worse, and then it stopped.

"Lou, this is Kelley. Can I come in?"

Lou got up and went to the door. He opened the door. Sergeant Kelley and Bobbi came in. Lou shut and locked the door.

"Hi, boss. Did you see the morning paper? Good morning, Lilly."

"Good morning, Brian. Good morning, Bobbi. Coffee?"

Bobbi went to Lilly and hugged her. "You bet I do."

"Sit down and tell us what is going on. I'll get your coffee."

The four sat down and sipped the coffee.

"Good coffee," said Bobbi.

"I can fix some eggs if you're hungry," Lilly added.

Bobbi laughed. "Tell them, Kelley."

"Stan Mason went to Washington and tried to get the Pentagon interested in the silver can. He had no proof, and they brushed him off. So he went to CNN, CBS, and newspapers and anyone who would listen. He put it on the internet."

"What is Stan saying?" asked Lou.

"Stan mentions you and Tim. He tells everything he knows about the can. It can make you smarter and healthier. It cures arthritist to every other known illness and disease. However, Stan did not say how dangerous it was or how many people died because of it."

"Well, Stan got someone to listen and believe," Lou said as he reached over and held Lilly's hand.

"Some reporters asked around town, and rumors came out of the closet. Kids at school told them about Tim and how he had changed. This all gave some credit to Stan's story," added Bobbi.

"We need to talk with Tim and his family. I'll call Jacob Weinstein."

"Lou, I tried that and even drove by his office and his home. He has vanished. There were people and news crews at both his office and his home," said Kelley.

"Ahhhh, Lilly would you like to cook up some more eggs? I think better on a full stomach."

"Yes, how about you two?" asked Lilly.

"Okay," answered Bobbi.

"Me too," answered Kelley.

CHAPTER 5-3

STAN MASON

Police siriens got everyone's attention. Lou and Kelley left the table and looked out the window. Four police squad cars stopped in front of Lou's house. Uniformed police officers took over crowd control. Chief Gibson could be seen walking to Lou's front door.

"I'll let him in," Kelley said as he walked to and opened the door.

The chief walked in.

"Good morning. Your nieghbors have reported a riot. How is everyone?"

Lou walked over to the chief.

"Come in, Chief. Kelley has been filling us in on the news," said Lou.

"Coffee, Chief?"

"Sure, thanks, Lilly."

Lilly puts another cup on the table and fills it with coffee. The chief picks it up and remains standing. He walks to the window and takes a long look.

"I think the crowd is under control and backed up to the curb."

"What is Stan Mason up to?" asked Bobbi.

"I thought he was going to back off. But I was wrong. I had a short conversation with him at the hospital," answered Lou.

"Is it greed?" asked Bobbi.

"Stan wants to be important. At least that had been my impression of him," added the chief.

"I wonder how Tim and his family are doing," commented Lilly.

"I don't know, Lilly, and I don't know how far out of control this silver can theory has spread. Stan wanted to use the can as a weapon."

"Gee, Lou," added Bobbi. "If Stan put it on the web, it could be all over the world. Who knows what kind of nuts will show up."

"I'm going to leave two squad cars here for your protection. I want Lilly and you to be safe, Lou."

"Thanks, Chief," said Lou. "I think Lilly and I are going to pack a few things and leave town. Our plane and hotel reservations for our honeymoon are not until late next week."

"I know a place," Kelley said. "I have an uncle who has a cabin. It's not too far from here. He uses it for hunting. I went there many times whe I was young. I can call him."

Lou looked at Lilly.

"It's up to you, Lou. You know better than me in these matters."

"Make the call, Kelley," Lou said.

Kelley got out his cell phone and walked out of the kitchen for a little privacy.

"I think that is the best thing to do. Hopefully, this will blow over," said the chief.

"I'll help you pack, Lilly," said Bobbi. "You better dress warm. Could be cold at this cabin."

"Okay, Bobbi," Lilly said, and the two women left the room.

"Lou, you don't think Stan would go to a foreign country with the can, do you?"

"I don't think he would do that, Chief. I am more worried about Stan becoming a super patriot and starting his little branch of the US Marines."

Kelley came back into the kitchen, nodding his head yes.

"It's all set if you want to do go to the cabin. Chief, I better go with them. We don't know what kind of problems they are going to run into, and I will have to show them the way. Plus I would be added security."

"What do you think, Lou?" asked the chief.

There was a knock on the door. Kelley went and opened the door. They whispered, and Kelley came back to the kitchen.

"There are some people, mostly men, digging in the woods out back."

Lou laughed. Chief Gibson's phone rang.

"Hello." He paused. "Okay. Send a squad right away," the chief said. "The crowd is getting larger and harder to control."

"I'll go pack a few things. What about you, Kelley? Are you going to need to get a few things?"

"I'll rough it. How are we going to get out of here without being followed?"

"If I ever see Stan again, I'm going to break his nose. Is it too late to file charges?" asked Lou.

"I'll give you a police escort out of town and then have the escort block the road for thirty minutes," said the chief, ignoring Lou's question.

"Sounds like a plan, Chief. I'll get ready," said Lou as he disappeared into the bedroom.

Lilly walked into the kitchen with a small bag.

"I'm ready," spoke Lilly.

Kelley went to the back door and looked out. He came back to the kitchen.

"Chief, there must be one hundred people out back digging in the woods."

"We better get going. Lou, are you ready?" yelled the chief.

"I'm ready," Lou said. "Kelley, you drive my car. Here are the keys."

Out the door they went. Kelley led the way. Behind him were Lou and Lilly. Bobbi and the chief were in the rear. When the people saw Lou, the crowd broke through the police line. The people were trying to touch Lou.

"Heal my child, please!" yelled one man.

"Help us! My wife is sick!" yelled another man.

"Save me! Please save me!" yelled a woman.

There was a lot of pushing and yelling, but Lou and Lilly were now safe in the car with Kelley behind the wheel. Bobbi fell. Kelley lost sight of the chief. Kelley jumped out of the car and pushed some people back. He picked up Bobbi as the mob moved toward them. Lou got out and helped Kelley get Bobbi into the back seat with Lilly. Kelley finally got behind the wheel, with Lou, Lilly, and Bobbi in the back seat. Kelley could not use the driveway. The mob was blocking the way to the road. Kelley saw an opening and took it, across the lawn, and behind the house where the Williams once lived.

Kelley cut across the lawns and made it back to the road. The four-car police escort caught up to them, and down the road, they sped.

"I hope the chief is all right. How are you, Bobbi?" asked Kelley.

"I'm all right. The mob knocked me down and walked right over me. Thanks for helping me."

Kelley drove, and once they were out of town, the escort stopped and blocked the road. Kelley kept checking to make sure no one was following.

CHAPTER 5-4

THE CABIN

Kelley finally pulled off the main highway and took some back roads. The back roads turned into dirt roads and, eventually, a narrow one-lane pathway though the woods. The cabin came into view; it was a small building with a porch and an outhouse on the far right.

The four went into the cabin.

"I see it has all the comforts of home," remarked Bobbi.

"It is charming, isn't it?" said Lilly.

"Excuse me," said Kelley. "I'll start the generator."

Kelley reached into a drawer and pulled out a flashlight. Then he went over by the back window and opened a trap door in the floor. Kelley went down the ladder, and in a few minutes, the generator came on and the cabin room lit up. Kelley came back up and closed the trap door.

"There is a vent for the fumes, and you will get used to the hum after a while. We better check for supplies."

Now, with the lights on, Lou looked at the inside of the cabin. There was a table, some chairs, a coffee table, a couch, some cupboards, a stove, a refrigerator, and a sink in the main room. There were two small bedrooms on the right and a fireplace on the left.

"We do have running water, but it is not to drink. I will go to town and get some supplies."

Bobbi went into one of the bedrooms.

"I found the the drinking water. Five cases of bottled water."

"We have a gas stove and a few space heaters. I'll start a fire in the fireplace. That will warm this place up. My uncle would appreciate a donation toward the cost of things if we survive whatever is going on in the world."

Lou pulled out his cell phone. He could not get a signal.

"I can't get a signal on my phone. I think the best thing is to try to get in touch with Tim. How does this work? Can he call me if I can't get a signal?"

"Kelley, is there a place I could stay in town where I could take Lou's phone and get a signal?" asked Bobbi. "I would wait there in case Tim tries to call."

"We will find something. What do you think, Lou?" asked Kelley.

Kelley had a fire going, and the heat from the fireplace began to warm up the cabin.

"We do need to stay in touch with the chief. Bobbi can do that, and maybe Tim will call. Thank God I remembered to bring that thing so you can charge it. Here, Bobbi."

Bobbi took Lou's phone and got ready to go.

"I'll be back in an hour. Are you ready, Bobbi?"

"Take care you two," Bobbi said, and then she gave Lilly a hug. And then Kelley and Bobbi left.

Lou reached into his pocket and squeezed the stone-like thing that the alien gave him. It was past time to be rid of the silver can.

"Alone at last," said Lilly.

Lou and Lilly sat cuddled on the couch in front of the fire.

"This is nice. You and I are alone by the fire."

"That's right, Lilly, and there is no one I would rather be with than you."

Lilly and Lou started kissing. There was a knock on the door. Lou jumped up and pulled out his gun. He went to the door.

"Who is it?"

"My name is Dr. Dunn. I am lost. Can you help me?"

Lou opened the door just a crack to see the man who called himself Dr. Dunn. He had on shorts and a tank top. Lou opened the door and did not see anyone else around.

"Come in and get warm. Lilly, get a blanket for this man. You must be cold, Dr. Dunn."

Dr. Dunn went into the cabin. Lilly gave him a blanket.

"Come and sit by the fire, Dr. Dunn," said Lilly. "Why are you dressed like you are, Dr. Dunn?"

"Lilly, give the man a break. I bet he was on his way to the outbuilding and did not expect to be gone long."

"That's right, and I got turned around somehow. I could not find my way back to my cabin."

"Do you know what way you came?" asked Lilly.

"I am from the city, and in the woods, it all looks the same," said Dr. Dunn.

"We are not much help, but there is someone who will be here soon that can help you," said Lilly. "We are new to the area, Dr. Dunn. I wish I had some hot food or a hot drink to offer you. We do have bottled water if you want a drink of that."

"Water would be good."

"I have some clothes that are warmer than what you have on. They may be a little baggy on you, but you are welcome to them."

"That would be nice. You are Lou, and the lady is Lilly. Is that right?"

"Yes, I am sorry. I am Lou Cameron, and this is my wife, Lilly. Are you alone, Dr. Dunn?" asked Lou.

"Yes, please call me Doc. I'm not a doctor, doctor. It's a title I ended up with because I have a docorate in ancient history."

"I like Doc. It is more friendly and personable," said Lilly.

"Can I take you up on the change of clothes?"

"Right in the bedroom on the right is a gray bag. Help yourself," said Lou.

Doc went into the bedroom and closed the door. Lou heard a car door slam. He got up and looked. Kelley was walking toward the cabin. He had two plastic bags of groceries. Lou opened the door, and Kelley set the bags on the table. Lilly started putting the food in the proper places. When Doc walked out of the bedroom, Kelley pulled his gun.

"Hold it right there," commanded Kelley.

"At ease, Sergeant. This is Dr. Dunn. He was lost and knocked on our door."

Kelley held his gun on the stranger.

"Where are you from?" asked Kelley.

The man did not answer.

"He said he went to the outhouse and lost his way back to his cabin," said Lilly.

"There is not another cabin for miles. My uncle owns this whole section, so I believe this man is not truthful. What is your name?"

"Dr. Thomas Dunn."

"Why are you here?"

The sound of a chopper interrupted the thoughts of everyone in the room.

"How did they find us?" asked Kelley.

"We don't have much time," said Dr. Dunn. "I came for the spoola."

"The spoola? What is that?" asked Kelley.

"It is what you call the silver can. We do not have much time. I know from the sound that the chopper is a US government chopper. They want the spoola."

"Sergent Kelley, it's okay. I met Dr. Dunn in Arizona," said Lou.

"Are you a spaceman, Dr. Dunn?" asked Lilly.

Lou and Kelley gave a quick look at Lilly.

"Some of your kind call me that."

"You are not of this world?" asked Lilly.

"True, we do not have a lot of time."

"That's a good point," Lou said. "Quickly, tell them what you want with the silver can."

"I want to take it back where it belongs, safe and secure, where no one on this planet can get hurt."

"We want it to be gone too. It has been nothing but trouble," said Lou.

"We can work together to get the spoola back where it belongs," said Dr. Dunn. "Before more of your kind dies."

"I say we trust Dr. Dunn," said Lilly.

"Well, we know what the government wants to do with the spoola, so I agree with Lilly. What about you, Kelley?"

"I need more proof. He could be a Russian and wants the silver can for a weapon for his country. Prove you're an alien."

"You want me to do some kind of a trick?"

"Do something to make me believe."

"We do not have time for this."

"Dr. Dunn is right, Kelley. We have to get out of here now," Lou said more forcefully.

"Okay, let's go. I'll turn off the generator."

Kelley put his weapon away and opened the trap door, and he went down the ladder. The generator stopped, and Kelley came back up the ladder. And the four of them started out the door.

"It's too late," said Lou. "They are here."

Lou closed the front door.

"Hide down in the hole in the floor," said Dr. Dunn. "I will pull the couch over the door and make a run out back."

Lou and Lilly went down first followed by Kelley. The stranger saw the food still in the platic bags. He quickly picked them up and handed them down to Kelly.

"There is an ecape door to the outside. We will wait until dark and try to leave," Kelley told Dr. Dunn.

"Okay, I will be waiting."

"How are you going to get away?" asked Kelley.

"Space magic."

Dr. Dunn then closed the door in the floor and moved the couch over the door. He then left the back door open and ran off in the woods.

Soldiers surrounded the cabin. They opened the front door and seached the building.

There was a lot of sounds coming from above, and then an "All clear" could be heard by Lou, Lilly, and Kelley. The three stood in silence.

"Major Smith, we must have just missed them. They could not have gone far. Their car is still here, and we found a suitcase and a duffel bag of clothes and personal belongings."

"Okay, Captain, have your men search the area."

"Yes, sir. Let's go, men. Seach the perimiter."

"Well, Stan, I think we should have them soon."

"You won't regret this, Major. The silver can will work miracles."

Kelley and Lou recognized Stan Mason's voice. Lou and Lilly held each other as they stood silently in the dark. Kelley had a flashlight but was afraid to use it. He felt around carefully until he found the handle to the small ecape door to the outside. Now all they had to do was wait until dark.

"Captain."

"Yes, Major Smith, did you find them?"

"No, sir. Some of the men saw a dog out back, and that is all."

"Captain, keep six men here at the cabin in case they return. Expand the search. When it's dark, we will have to call off the search and start again in the morning. Stan and I are going back to town."

"Yes, sir. Good night, sir."

The three hidden in the floor could hear the footsteps of the men leaving and then the quiet silence. Kelley cracked open the escape door to the outside. It was still too light outside. There were sounds of the military vehicles engines starting and doors slamming. Then there was the sound of the trucks and cars moving away from the cabin.

Then there were some voices from inside the cabin.

"Anything to report, Sergeant?"

"No, sir. All we have seen is a stray dog hanging around. Sir, some of the men want to send someone to town and get some pizzas. It would be better than this canned military food."

"I agree with you, Sergeant. When it gets dark, we will send one man into town. I do not think these people we are looking for will return tonight. I think they are in the next county by now."

It was dark now, and Kelley opened the ecape door. Lou, Lilly, and Kelley stepped out into the darkness. Dr. Dunn was standing there, waiting.

"Shhh, this way," he whispered.

The small group sneaked away from the cabin and toward the outhouse. Lilly grabbed Lou's arm and whispered to him.

"Wait a minute," Lou whispered. "Lilly needs to use the outhouse."

The group stopped, and Lilly carefully opened the door and went inside. Kelley and Lou both relieved themselves outside. Lilly came out, and they walked to the narrow lane to the cabin. They heard the sound of the truck start up.

"I'll stop the vehicle, and you three get in the back," whispered Dr. Dunn. "That vehicle is going to take us to town."

There was no time to discuss the plan or ask how Dr. Dunn was going to stop the truck. Kelly, Lou, and Lilly hid behind some trees, and when the army truck stopped, Lou and Kelley helped Lilly get in the back. And then they both climbed in the vehicle.

"Get out of the way, dog," yelled the driver. The dog did not move, and the driver opened his door and got out. Then the dog ran away.

"Damn dog," yelled the driver as he gots back in the truck.

Dr. Dunn appeared at the back of the truck and climbed inside, and the vehicile moved toward town.

CHAPTER 5-5

THE SEARCH FOR TIM

The army truck pulled into town and stopped in front of a pizza place. The driver got out and went inside. Lou, Lilly, Kelley, and Dr. Dunn get out the back and slipped into the shadows of the alley.

"Lou, you better stay out of sight. I'll go and find Bobbi and find out if she has heard from Tim," said Kelley.

"Okay, Kelley, hurry back. Lilly, are you warm enough?"

"I am a little chilled, Lou."

"We need some jackets or something to keep Lilly and me warm. How about you, Dr. Dunn?"

"I am all right. Are you in touch with Tim?"

"I will be pretty soon," said Lou.

As Kelley was walking away, a local police car pulled into the alley and turned on the flashing lights. A tall man got out of the squad car and walked toward the group.

"What's going on here? I saw you get out of the truck and run into the alley."

"Johnny, is that you?" asked Kelley.

"Brian, what's going on? I'm surprised to see you."

"Johnny, could you turn off the flashing lights? I'll explain everything." Kelley then turned to Lou, Lilly, and the stranger. "Johnny is my cousin. His father owns that cabin we were in."

"Okay, Brian."

Johnny was younger than Brian but taller and leaner. He turned off the flashing lights.

"Brian, it has been a few years. How is life in the big city? You still a cop?"

"Yes, John, and I am trying to protect these people, and I sure could use your help."

"Okay, Brian. What do you need?"

"We need a ride to some place safe where we can talk."

"Okay, everyone get in the car, and we will go somewhere and talk."

"We have to stop at the Starlite Motel. We have a fellow officer there that may have some information that we need."

"I'll help you as much as I can, Brian. You are the reason I am a cop."

"Thanks, Johnny."

They went down the road. Johnny was driving, and Kelley was in the front. Lou and Lilly rode in the back seat with Dr. Dunn.

"Johnny, the man behind you is Detective Lou Cameron. The lady with him is his wife, Lilly. This other man is Dr. Dunn. He is on our side."

"Call me Doc," said Dr. Dunn.

"Dectective Lou Cameron, I read about you in the paper and saw your picture on the news. Is this all about that silver can?"

"That's right, Johnny," said Lou.

The squad car pulled into the motel, and Kelley disappeared into one of the rooms. Kelley soon returned with Bobbi, who slid in the front seat between Johnny and Kelley.

"Where to now?" asked Johnny.

"Take us somewhere safe, and we can talk."

"A warm place, please," said Lilly.

"Who do we have with us?" asked Bobbi.

"Bobbi, this is Officer John Kelley. He is my cousin. You know Lou and Lilly, and the stranger in the back is called Doc. He helped us ecape from the cabin."

"He helped you ecape from what? The people? The media?"

"The US Army."

"The US Army?" asked Johnny and Bobbi at the same time.

"It's a long story," said Kelly.

The car pulled into a driveway.

"Home sweet home. My wife is visiting her mother, so let's go in. We can all tell our story."

They all went inside and and sat in the living room. It was an old country house. The rooms were large with high ceilings.

"Johnny, could we see what you have to eat? I don't mean to be rude, but Kelley, Lou, and I have not eaten in a long time," asked Lilly.

Without saying a word, Johnny led them to the kitchen.

"Please, help yourself."

"I'll help you, Lilly," said Bobbi.

The two women started looking in the cupboards and the fridge.

"Eggs and toast anyone?" asked Lilly.

"Sounds good to me," said Lou.

"Me too," said Kelley.

Lilly started frying eggs. Bobbi set the table. Johnny made the toast. Lou decided it was time to take command.

"Let me have everyone's attention. Apologies to my lovley wife, Lilly, and Sergeant Kelley. Dr. Dunn and I tried putting on a charade. Dr. Dunn and I met last week in Arizona, soon after Lilly was shot. We had hoped to work together to get the silver can or what Dr. Dunn calls a spoola back in Dr. Dunn's possesion. We had planned to tell as few people as possible. But Stan Mason went and told the world about the can, and now the cat is out of the bag."

"What are you telling us, Lou?" asked Bobbi.

"Lou, let me try to explain," said Dr. Dunn. "My name is not Dr. Dunn, but Dr. Dunn is easier for humans to pronounce. Last spring, I was on a mission to recover some bodies of my species and return them to my home planet."

"What?" Bobbi and Johnny asked.

"I am responsible for bringing the spoola, or what you call the silver can, to your planet. We did not know we had lost a spoola until we took inventory back on our home planet. We knew we had to recover it because it is very dangerous. A spoola radiates a chemical that can kill humans. We had a faulty bacda that let one of our spoola's slip out. Now we are on a mission to recover the spoola."

"Where did you lose this thing?" asked Johnny.

"The Arizona desert. Sheriff Justin Smith, the sheriff out there, has been a great help. He understands and has seen the the death and the greed that has followed the spoola. The deaths at the MPL company in Austin was our first clue, and then that left us wondering where to go next."

"You are a spaceman from another world?" asked Bobbi.

"Yes, Bobbi. Doc is a spaceman. Close your mouth, dear. Eat some eggs," said Lilly.

Dr. Dunn paused for a moment. "We are a race of explorers. We have no intention to invade or cause any problems, but we have, over the years, done things that have affected your planet."

"Doc, why were you wearing the clothes you had on when I first met you?" asked Lilly.

"That is all I had for human clothing. I do not look like you. I have learned how to make myself look human."

"I do not believe this," said Johnny.

"I believe it. I believe it all," said Kelley.

"Me too," said Bobbi.

"Sheriff Smith and his wife and a few others monitored the news. That is how we found Lou. And Lou, you have been a great help because Tim has agreed to return the spoola."

"Johnny, I know this is a lot to take in and understand," Lou said. "We had a mob at Lilly's and my home this morning. People are crazy about the can. They think it is the answer to all their problems."

A phone rang, and the room became quiet. Bobbi pulled out Lou's phone.

"Hello, Tim. We have been waiting for your call. This is Bobbi. Yes, he is right here." Bobbi handed the phone to Lou.

"Tim, yes." He paused. "I know." He paused again. "We had a mob at our house this morning, and the US Army is after us. They want the can."

Lilly looked at Bobbi and Johnny. The room was quiet.

"Jacob Weinstein is talking with the govenor. Tim and his family are in Brunswick. Weinstein has a summer home there. Tim would like to meet you, Doc. Tim says your spoola is in a safe place. If it is possible, Tim wants to meet and talk with you, Dr. Dunn. Tim, it may not be possible at this time because we have everyone looking for us. Our priority is the spoola. Okay, Tim, we should see you soon. Goodbye."

Johnny cleared his throat. "How can you prove the can belongs to Dr. Dunn?"

Dr. Dunn stood there, thinking. "There is some small code on the bottom of the spoola. Lou, give me a paper and pencil."

Lou gave Dr. Dunn a paper and pencil, and Dr. Dunn made some marks on the paper.

"This is my written lanuage, and the same symbols will appear on the spoola."

"It could be a trick. I want to be sure," said Johnny.

"I understand, Johnny. Life or death are the results of the decisions that we make here tonight, in this room, in this house. Your house, Johnny. I do not have an army to fight the US Army if they get control of the spoola. I do not have enough space magic or firepower to fight them or the Russians. All I have are the people in this room and Tim. The safe recovery of the spoola will keep balance in the world."

"Johnny, I believe Doc," said Lou. "The sooner we get rid of the spoola, the better off we are. We have to meet Tim tomorrow."

"Lou, the can did bring us together," said Lilly.

Lou reached out and touched Lilly's hand.

"Yes, Lilly is right about that. Unfortunately, there are those that want to use it as a weapon."

"Is that why the army is after you?" asked Johnny.

"Yes," answered Lou. "Johnny we are going to need some transportation."

Johnny nodded his head yes and looked at his watch.

"I should check in. I am on duty till six a.m."

Johnny disappeared into another room.

Doc looked at Kelley. "Can you trust him?"

Kelley got up and followed Johnny.

"Doc, if you get the spoola, will you be able to get it on your spaceship and go back to your home? Will there be any problems?"

"That depends on how it goes and the US Army."

There was a crash coming from the room where Johnny and Kelley went. Lou jumped up and ran to where the sound came. Bobbi, Lilly, and Dr. Dunn were behind Lou. Kelley had Johnny on the floor, lying on his belly.

"He was calling the FBI. Lou, help me cuff him," Kelley said. Then Kelley looked at Dr. Dunn. "How did you know?"

"I can tell when a human lies. It's a gift."

The group looked at Dr. Dunn in disbelief. There was a quiet moment when it started to sink in that Dr. Dunn was who he said he was. Kelley got Johnny to his feet.

"He could be a Russian. So what if he writes some symbols on a paper? They could be Russian symbols."

"Lilly how are the eggs doing?" asked Lou.

Lilly and Bobbi ran back to the kitchen. Kelley brought Johnny in the kitchen and sat him down.

"What did he say to the FBI?" asked Lou.

"He said, 'Is this the FBI? I want to report—,' and then I jumped him."

"Good work, Kelley," said Lou. "We have to leave."

"What are we going to do with Johnny?" asked Kelley.

"We have to bring him. Brunwick is where we have to to go to meet Tim."

"You'll never get away with this!" Johnny cried. "They will catch you."

Lou grabbed the dishrag and stuffed it in Johnny's mouth.

"Up to now, we have not broken any laws. Now, we have assaulted a police officer, and when we drive off in his car, grand theft auto will be on our records."

"I had such high hopes for you, Johnny," said Kelley.

"Let's eat and hit the road," said Lou. After they ate, Lou said, "Hit the bathroom if you need too. We have a long ride ahead of us. Kelley, you drive. Ladies in the front, and Doc and I will watch Johnny in the back. Okay? Let's go, people."

"I love it when Lou takes over," said Lilly.

"Me too," said Bobbi.

CHAPTER 5-6

HOLD YOUR FIRE

The stolen police car was traveling toward Brunswick in the dark of night.

"Someone will be looking for this squad car," Kelley said.

"They probably are right now. I wish Tim would call," said Lou.

"I have Weinstein's number in my phone. Bobbi, take it and see IF he will answer."

Bobbi took Kelley's phone and made the call.

"Hello, Jacob Weinstein?" She paused. "Yes, my name is Officer Bobbi Jackson. I am with Dectective Cameron. We need to reach Tim." Bobbi then ended the call.

"What happened, Bobbi?" asked Kelley.

"I left a message."

Lou looked at Johnny.

"Johnny, we want you on our side. We are trying to save the world, believe it or not. Your cousin, Kelley, is one of the best."

"What would your father say about you betraying me?" asked Kelley. "Our fathers were brothers. You and I have been like brothers. You have to trust me on this and have some faith in me."

Lou took the washrag out of Johnny's mouth. Johnny spat, trying to clear out the taste of the washrag.

"All right, I will trust you," says Johnny.

"I am not a Russian. I want to help your planet. If we remove the handcuffs, will you cause trouble?" asks Dr. Dunn.

Johnny sat there, thinking.

"Okay, I did not want to do this, but I know we have some doubters here. I can turn myself into a dog. Will that prove anything?"

"I'd like to see that," said Kelley as he pulled the car over to the side of the road.

With the car stopped and everyone watching, Dr. Dunn turned into a dog. After everyone had a good look, the dog turned into Dr. Dunn. There was a moment of silence.

"I will cause no trouble," said Johnny.

Lou looked at Dr. Dunn.

"Is he telling the truth?"

"I am telling the truth," said Johnny.

"Yes, he is telling the truth," reaffirmed Dr. Dunn.

Kelley got the car back on the road. Lou uncuffed Johnny.

"Dr. Dunn, do you need to contact your spaceship? I feel so silly asking a question like that. Spaceships and aliens and all that—I would have called it hogwash until now."

"Lou, I am in constant communications with my crew."

Day broke, and the sun started to light up the world. The phone rang, and they heard the sound of sirens.

"We have company," Kelley said.

"Do not stop," Lou tells Kelley. "Hello, Tim. (pause) We have trouble. The State Police are following us. The sirens are blasting, and the lights are flashing."

"I hear a chopper," says Kelley.

Bobbi's phone rang. She answered it. She talked low so she wouldn't disturb Lou.

"Tim, we are on Route 65. Tim, you have to trust me on that. We will be a lot safer if Dr. Dunn takes the silver can back to where it belongs. You are not having secound thoughts, are you? We have cop cars chasing us. We have a helicopter flying over head."

"Lou, let me talk to Tim," said the stranger. Lou handed the phone to Dr. Dunn. "Tim, it is now or never. Good. Tim, do you have the can?

Okay, can you come down Route 65? When you get to a big open field, run to the far end, away from the road. Take the can with you. What is the can in right now? A plastic ziplock bag, perfect. You stand by the edge of the woods, and when we see you, we will stop. I will meet you there. Stay on the phone with Lou."

"That call was from Jacob Weinstein. He has talked with the governor about our situation. The two of them are trying to end this madness."

"See, someone is on our side," said Lilly.

"Tim says he found a field and is running to the far end. What side of the road are you on, Tim? Our right. Okay, everyone, see if you can spot Tim."

"We have ten or more cop cars following us. That is an army chopper. I would bet that Stan Mason is in the helicopter," said Kelley.

"Tim says the police have set up a roadblock and have his dad and mom in custody."

"There he is," yelled Johnny.

Kelley stopped the car.

"Lou, tell Tim to go into the woods," Dr. Dunn said as he got out of the car.

"Tim, go into the woods. Dr. Dunn will meet you there."

Someone fired a shot. Then it sounded like everyone opened fire. Tim went down and was still. Kelley, Lou, and Bobbi jumped out of the car.

"HOLD YOUR FIRE! STOP SHOOTING!" the three of them yelled.

The gunfire ceased. The police took Kelley, Lou, and Bobbi in custody. Johnny and Lilly got out of the car and watched where Tim lay. Some of the police officers started walking across the field. There were newspeople there. Another helicopter came in view. CNN NEWS was printed in big letters on its side.

"He's alive. He's alive. Lilly, he's alive," Johnny whispered to Lilly.

Tim got up and ran into the woods. Tim did not get far, but he was out of sight. Tim lay there on his belly.

"Tim, I am Dr. Dunn. Put the bag with the can in my mouth," whispered a voice.

Tim rolled on his side and held up the bag. A golden retriever bit down on the edge of the ziplock bag and winked with one eye at Tim and then disappeared. Within minutes, Tim was surrounded by police.

"He doesn't have a weapon, sir," said a cop talking on his radio. "No, I don't see no silver can. Sir, get a helicopter in this field. The young man needs to go to the hospital right away."

CHAPTER 5-7

SAFE AT LAST

The helicopter with Tim aboard left for the hospital. A dark, shiny new car pulled up to where Lou and the others were. Two men got out of the car. The governor and Jacob Weinstein walked over to one of the police officers.

"Who's in charge here?" asked Weinstein.

No one answered.

"Why are these people handcuffed?"

One of the officers answered, "We were chasing a stolen police car."

"It was not stolen. It is mine," spoke up Johnny. "I am Officer John Kelley, and I was trying to protect these people from an angry mob."

"I think you should release these people right now. They have not broken any laws," said Weinstein.

A police officer finally came over.

"I'm Captain Renner with the state police. Officer, release these people."

"Thank you, sir. Those two people over there need to be released also."

"Release them, Officer." Then Captain Renner turned to the governor and tipped his cap. "Okay, I need to know who fired their weapons."

"Let's get out of here," Lou said. "Thanks, Mr. Weinstein. Can you find out where they are taking Tim?"

"I will find out," Weinstein said as he walked over to the governor. The governor made a call and turned to Weinstein.

"Saint Luke's. You can follow us."

"Thank you!" yelled Lou.

"Let's go!" yelled Johnny. "I'll drive."

They piled into Johnny's police car, and Lou saw Ray and Stella get in the governor's car. The two cars went to Saint Luke's Hospital. The media was waiting outside the hospital. Lou and his group pushed their way through the crowd. Ray, Stella, the governor, and Jacob Weinstein were waiting inside.

Weinstein talked to the front desk, and Weinstein went over to Ray and Stella. After speaking with Weinstein, Ray went over to Lou.

"Tim is in surgery," a nervous and upset Ray told Lou. "Thanks for coming."

The governor left, and the rest of the group went to the waiting room. It was not long, and a doctor came out and talked with Ray and Stella. Stella started crying, and Ray could be seen comforting her. Jacob Weinstein went over to Lou.

"We are going to have a news conference at noon. Tim did not make it. I want you to speak at the news conference. We are taking the stand that it was all a hoax—the imagination of a fourteen-year-old. Then maybe we can have some peace. 'There never was a can' is what I am going to say."

Stan Mason and Major Smith came down the hall.

"How is the boy doing?" asked Stan.

"As if you care," remarked Bobbi as she stood up and started walking toward Stan. Kelley grabbed and restrained Bobbi.

"Get out of here, Stan," remarked Lou. "Tim did not make it."

"We are sorry for your loss," said Major Smith.

"Where is the silver can?" asked Stan.

"Stan, there is no can. Now get out of here, or I'll throw you out."

"Stan, let's go," said Major Smith. "Sorry, folks. My prayers are with you."

Major Smith and Stan left the way they came. Another doctor came out and asked, "Who wants to see the body?"

"I think we all do," said Ray.

Ray, Stella, Lou, Kelley, Bobbi, Johnny, Lilly, and Weinstein all followed the doctor down the hall to a private room. Tim lay there on his back with his eyes closed. The group of eight went to where Tim's body lay. The door shut behind them.

Tim sat up and said, "I hope you all can keep a secret."

*   *   *

The theme song for CNN news came on. "Hello, this is Wayne Gibbs for CNN with the one o'clock news. The mystery of the silver can is over. In a news conference at noon today, Jacob Weinstein, a lawyer representing the Tim Williams family, made the announcement that Tim Williams was shot and killed.

The police believed that Williams had in his possession the silver can that was rumored to cure all kinds of diseases. There was no silver can found. Weinstein and Detective Louis Cameron denied there was a can and said it was all a hoax made up by Tim Williams. Tim Williams was fourteen years old. In other news, the president said today . . ."

THE END

CPSIA information can be obtained
at www.ICGtesting.com
Printed in the USA
BVHW081806180319
542953BV00008B/169/P

9 781796 019810